'How do you do, Mr Seton?' she said, deliberately emphasising the formal address.

Warm, strong fingers enclosed hers in a quite unnecessarily strong grasp. He poured more charm into his smile. '"She was a phantom of delight, when first she gleamed upon my sight . . ."'

'You surprise me, Mr Seton . . . quoting a romantic poet like Wordsworth,' she mocked. Her eyes blazed with scorn at his attempt to sweet-talk her. 'And, apart from anything else, it is not accurate. I am certainly not a phantom.'

'Nor would I wish you to be, Antonia,' was the smooth rejoinder, his eyes dancing with pleasure and a very definite glint of sexual anticipation.

Toni fumed. 'No one except Ray calls me Antonia. All my friends call me Toni. You, Mr Seton, may call me Miss Braden.'

ONE-WOMAN CRUSADE

BY

EMMA DARCY

MILLS & BOON LIMITED
ETON HOUSE   18-24 PARADISE ROAD
RICHMOND   SURREY   TW9 1SR

First published in Great Britain 1990 by Mills & Boon Limited

© Emma Darcy 1990

Australian copyright 1990 Philippine copyright 1990 This edition 1990

ISBN 0 263 76736 1

Set in Times Roman 10½ on 11½ pt. 01-9007-52983 C

Made and printed in Great Britain

To Karen—
for her care
and understanding

CHAPTER ONE

TONI BRADEN had never met Noah Seton. She had gone out of her way to avoid meeting him. Tonight, however, she had no excuse. It was a family party, and family always came first with Toni. No matter what.

Nevertheless, the fact that she had to meet him and pretend to be civil to him only increased Toni's inner outrage over what he had done. It was not the disruption that Noah Seton was causing in her own life. Not at all! She could cope easily enough with that. It was the fear and despair and dislocation he was creating in twenty-seven other lives that formed the basis of her furious discontent.

Somehow she had to rectify the situation. Already she had made some plans, and her mind slid over them before reverting to the cause of all the problems.

Noah Seton!

The very name was anathema to her. He had caused too much pain already to people who were near and dear to her. Take-overs were immoral, she thought fiercely. They should be declared illegal! And men like Noah Seton should be stripped of any respectability and shown up for the callous monsters that they were!

The thought gave Toni some remote satisfaction. Her agile mind swiftly reviewed her wide collection of friends and acquaintances who were in a position to achieve this eminently desirable result. Despite the fact that she knew a wide range of people in Sydney, and many in top-level professions, the only person who really sprang to mind was Diana Goldbach—a gossip columnist—who was too lightweight for Toni's purpose on this important matter.

Which meant she had to do something about it herself. And quickly! Time was fast running out. Constructive action was imperative. And if she got half a chance at this party tonight—no, she would make the chance—she would tackle Noah Seton about the situation he had caused. He could hardly escape her in her own home. Although confronting him with his inhumanity was almost certainly futile, he being the kind of man he was. She had to come up with some better idea than that.

She picked up the brightest red lipstick she owned and slashed it across her lips. How she would like to make that man bleed in the same way he was bleeding the heart out of people she had come to know and like over the last six years! Of course, the employees whose lives were drastically affected by the take-over meant nothing to Noah Seton. He was simply adding another transport company to his worldwide network. Never mind people like old Mr Templeton who didn't have a hope of re-careering himself when the new broom swept him out of his job. As had already happened. The fear and anxiety that had pervaded the company offices these last few weeks were too real for Toni to shrug off.

Never had she felt less like partying. The sense of indignation and outrage prompted by Noah Seton's unfeeling ruthlessness made the idea of partying almost obscene. Particularly in *his* company!

For all of her twenty-four years Toni had viewed life as a ball, and her aim had always been to extract as much fun out of it as she could. Even her brief foray into marriage had not dimmed her natural exuberance for long. She had shrugged that off as a useful and timely learning experience that she was lucky to get out of with no deep hurt to either side. But there was no fun in this company take-over by Noah Seton. The results were all too real. And Toni was brutally faced with the soul-hitting truth that skating through life was a privilege that few people could afford.

Yet, as much as she had protested at her stepfather's decision to sell his business, she couldn't really blame him for doing so. In purely financial terms the offer had been too good to refuse. And Raymond Clifford was ready to retire. But Toni certainly didn't feel like going downstairs to celebrate Noah Seton's newest acquisition. With the misery he was causing, there was no way in the world she could wish that man well.

Nevertheless, it was expected of her. Her stepfather expected it. Her stepsister expected it; indeed, Jocelyn insisted on it. And no doubt Noah Seton expected it too. The whole family was putting its best foot forward to encourage his supposed interest in Jocelyn. Although how her stepsister could fancy the idea of marrying a soulless person like Noah Seton was beyond Toni's imagination. It would be like marrying a computer.

She picked up her hairbrush and drove the hard bristles through the thick mass of black curls, forcing them back behind her ear so she could slide in the side-comb which would hold them there. They could tumble everywhere else as wildly as they liked, but she needed a bit of severity to offset the taffeta frill which trailed over one shoulder from the otherwise strapless bodice of her dress. If she had to go and meet that man, she would do it in style! Never let it be said that she let the family down!

All the same, she had mutinously decided to wear black. At least that was a statement of her feelings on the matter, however obscure it might be to anyone else. And no jewellery either! It would be disgustingly distasteful to sparkle when Noah Seton was casting such a blight over other people's lives.

Having savaged her hair into at least temporary order, Toni pushed herself up from the dressing-table and scrutinised her appearance in the cheval-mirror which was positioned near the door for a handy last-minute check. She scowled at the spoiling effect of the deep violet and emerald-green underfrills that gave a vividly dramatic feature to the black taffeta skirt, and peeped out from the ruffle over her shoulder. Why did she have to have such a weakness for rich colour? She didn't even have one classic little black dress in her whole wardrobe like any other sensible woman, and this was one time when her newly sensitised conscience couldn't possibly justify the extravagance of buying something new. Not now that she had been made so aware of the terrible sense of insecurity that a loss of regular income meant. This dress was as black as she had, so it would have to do.

With a disgruntled sigh, Toni dismissed her unsatisfactory reflection and set her mind to getting through this party with a semblance of equanimity. What had to be done had to be done, and it was totally pointless crying over spilt milk. Action was the answer to the problem. Quick, constructive action that would help everyone into new jobs. Better jobs!

And if Jocelyn was intent on making a disastrous marriage, that was Jocelyn's business. After her own little adventure into the matrimonial state, Toni was hardly in a position to make critical judgements of anyone's choice of a husband. Jocelyn was entitled to make one mistake. She had made hers.

However, Toni's well-meant resolution didn't get beyond the head of the staircase.

'Noah...' her stepfather's voice boomed up from the foyer below. He broke away from the group of guests still hovering at the entrance to the reception-room, and, with his hands outstretched in welcome, strode quickly towards the man who had just been admitted by the butler.

The Clifford household didn't normally have a formal butler, but no expense was being spared on this party tonight. Toni viewed the welcoming scene with stormy green eyes. All to impress Noah Seton, she seethed. And he probably wouldn't even notice half of it. Mega-millionaires like him were more interested in profitable numbers than anything else. He was thirty-six, Jocelyn had told her, which meant he had to be singularly ruthless to have made all the money he had. Mean and ruthless!

'Looks as if you've got quite a party here, Ray,' came the reply in a surprisingly pleasant voice, deep, but lightly pitched to convey warmth.

Toni didn't listen for her stepfather's undoubtedly modest demur. She was making a jaundiced inventory of Noah Seton's physical assets. He was slightly taller than her stepfather, which made him close to six feet in height. A formal dress-suit invariably flattered most men, but she had to concede that he had quite an impressive physique: broad shoulders tapering down to a lean waist. There was a fullness about his elegantly trousered legs that denied any weediness in that department. Definitely a virile-looking specimen.

His hair was thick and straight, almost as black as his suit, and styled to sweep across the high line of his forehead and tuck neatly around ears that—much to her chagrin—Toni couldn't take any exception to. However, his face wasn't particularly handsome, which was much more satisfactory. The angles of it were too hard with those high cheekbones, the strong nose, and a sharply defined jawline which had a squarish cut to it. His eyebrows had a distinctive kick with a late arch above the corners of his eyes, and they lent a certain wicked attractiveness to what was a very masculine face. All in all, Toni couldn't see what there was to make Jocelyn feel weak at the knees. If, in fact, she did.

As if some sixth sense alerted him to her angry scrutiny, he suddenly looked up at her. Despite her deep antagonism towards the man, Toni was jolted by the sheer magnetism he projected with that one sharp look. Somehow he diminished everything around him as if he were the only vital element worth acknowledging. He kept on staring at her with almost mesmerising force...eyes so dark that they looked black, but lit with an acute intelligence which seemed all-seeing and all-knowing.

'Ah...there you are, Antonia!' Her stepfather's voice held a mildly critical note. 'You're late coming down.'

Toni managed to tear her eyes away from Noah Seton's long enough to direct an apologetic reply. 'Am I, Ray? Sorry! I must have lost track of the time.' For his sake...for Jocelyn's sake...she had to pretend to be civil!

'Well, it looks like time well spent,' Ray said indulgently, slanting his smile up at the man who had broken off their conversation at sight of his stepdaughter.

Noah Seton was totally unaware of Ray Clifford's half-questioning smile. He was totally unaware of anything but the woman who was now descending the long, curving staircase to the foyer. She was not the most beautiful woman he had ever seen. He didn't even think of her as beautiful. She was such an intensely vivid entity that beauty was irrelevant. Energy seemed to vibrate from her . . . a turbulent, electric vitality that engulfed him, challenged him, stunned him. The sheer impact of her was totally riveting. For a moment there—at first sight of her—it had almost seemed that the earth had shaken under his feet.

It wasn't until she was standing in front of him that he recollected himself enough to notice physical detail: a wild profusion of tight black curls, straight wrathful eyebrows above green eyes that audaciously defied his interest, a delicate little nose that tilted with haughty pride, a mouth that flagrantly invited ravishment— the lower lip curved with sensual fullness, the upper lip provocatively bow-shaped—and a determined little chin, its belligerence undermined by the faint dimple in its centre.

Her face was turned up to his and he suddenly realised how small she was—a head shorter than himself even in high heels. That, too, was somehow surprising. His mind was stamped with the impression of intense female sexuality, a powerhouse of a woman who was larger than life, voluptuously curved and flauntingly feminine.

'Antonia, this is Noah Seton. My stepdaughter, Antonia Braden, Noah.'

Ray Clifford's introduction seemed to come from a far-away distance. Noah belatedly thrust out a hand

and forced a smile to his lips. 'I'm delighted to meet you, Antonia.'

Toni was struggling to contain a towering fury. She was incensed that this man should have stared so knowingly at her all the way down the stairs. Every step! It was disgusting—worse than stripping her naked. It was as if he could see into her very soul. He certainly needed putting in his place. She could barely bring herself to touch his hand. Politeness demanded it—particularly in front of her stepfather.

'How do you do, Mr Seton?' she said, deliberately emphasising the formal address. The idea of giving him a piece of her mind had firmed in the last few moments, and, with what she intended to say to him later, an icy approach was definitely called for.

Warm strong fingers enclosed hers in a quite unnecessarily strong grasp. It gave her a nasty trapped feeling. She did not return the pressure.

'I've been waiting a long time for this pleasure,' he said in his seductive, smiling voice.

'I've been waiting a long time for this pleasure, too,' she replied, and in one sense that was certainly true. Later on . . . Satisfaction might be dearly bought, but buy it she would . . . when the showdown came.

He poured more charm into his smile. ' "She was a phantom of delight, when first she gleamed upon my sight" . . .'

The words from the poem were so softly intoned that an odd quivery feeling ran through Toni. It was a lovely thing to say. But coming from him! Her outrage moved up a notch.

'You surprise me, Mr Seton . . . quoting a romantic poet like Wordsworth,' she mocked, letting him know that she knew those words didn't come from his soul. He undoubtedly had a memory like a computer too!

Her eyes blazed her scorn at his attempt to sweet-talk her. 'And, apart from anything else,' she added loftily, 'It is not accurate. I am certainly not a phantom.'

'Nor would I wish you to be, Antonia,' was the smooth rejoinder, his eyes dancing with pleasure and a very definite glint of sexual anticipation.

Toni fumed. He shouldn't be looking at her like that when he had come here to be with Jocelyn! The man had no sense of decency. No conscience at all. Toni's sense of discretion fled in the face of this further proof of his perfidy. If ever anyone needed to be taught a few lessons, Noah Seton was that person!

'No one except Ray calls me Antonia. All my friends call me Toni.' She offered him a smile that had been invented by Lucrezia Borgia as she poisoned her enemies. 'You, Mr Seton, may call me Miss Braden.'

A loaded little silence followed. For the first time he seemed lost for words. These small pin-pricks to his arrogance were definitely needed, Toni assured herself.

Then Jocelyn arrived on the scene. Which was probably very timely, considering the amount of dangerously heating steam that Toni was suppressing for her stepfather's sake. Noah Seton was still holding her hand in an infuriatingly possessive manner, and, short of staging an undignified tug of war with him, Toni couldn't see how to disengage it. She was more than happy for Jocelyn to claim him . . . for the time being.

'Have you been holding Noah up, talking business again, Dad?' Jocelyn chided good-humouredly as she wound her arm around Noah Seton's. This loosened his grip on Toni's hand and she quickly retrieved it.

Ray gave a laugh that was tinged with relief. 'Not at all, my dear. I was just performing introductions. You can take him away now.'

'He's all yours!' Toni added with feeling.

Jocelyn shot her an anxious look which begged a number of questions. Toni managed a reassuring smile, although she felt like a terrible hypocrite. Yet she couldn't help herself. It was second nature to her to save Jocelyn worry, no matter how serious the situation was. From the very beginning of their relationship her younger stepsister had brought out a strongly protective instinct in Toni. Although Jocelyn had overcome her stutter in her teens—her voice was beautifully modulated now—and there was no real reason for Toni to fight any more battles for her stepsister's sake, the instinct was still there.

'You look lovely, Jocelyn!' she rushed out with genuine sincerity, while mentally stabbing Noah Seton for not saying it.

'Beautiful . . . as always,' he came in on cue, having finally focused his attention on the woman who had invited him here.

It squeezed Toni's heart to see how his belated compliment literally illuminated Jocelyn's face with a beauty that was far more than skin-deep. Her stepsister deserved someone better than Noah Seton, someone who would love and cherish her for the rest of her life, and who would never look at another woman! Although why he was even tempted to was beyond Toni's comprehension. In her opinion, no other woman could hold a candle to Jocelyn.

She had a perfect face. Every feature was classically moulded, and those fascinating amber eyes could glow golden with warmth—as now. Even her hair was honey and gold, styled in a long silky fall which curled

softly around her shoulders. She was tall and wonderfully willowy, always looking supremely elegant in
anything she wore, and the bronze silk gown she had
chosen for tonight looked fabulous on her superbly
slim figure. She had set it off brilliantly with a gold
choker that only someone with Jocelyn's long,
graceful neck could have worn successfully.

Toni was not given to envy. Envy was a waste of
time which could be far better spent on doing whatever
could be done with her own life. But, if she had been
given a choice on her own physical construction, she
would have chosen Jocelyn as the ideal model. It
seemed positively perverse of Noah Seton to even
glance back at her now that Jocelyn had joined them.
But he did. Fixing those devilishly knowing black eyes
on hers in deliberate challenge.

'Are you coming with us to join the party . . . Miss
Braden?' he asked silkily.

Ray instantly placed a restraining hand on Toni's
arm. 'I want to have a private word with Antonia first.
You two go ahead.' He smiled benevolently. 'Enjoy
yourselves.'

'Don't be long with Toni, Dad,' Jocelyn warned,
throwing a happy grin at her older stepsister. 'Everyone's been asking where you are. No party really
begins without you, Toni.'

Noah Seton at least had the grace to go with Jocelyn
without further ado, and Toni succumbed to her stepfather's hand-pressure and was drawn into the library
on the other side of the foyer.

'That wasn't very friendly, Antonia,' he started as
soon as the door was safely shut behind them. 'I know
you're upset by the take-over, but Noah Seton is a
guest in our house and——'

'He was the first to be rude!' Toni broke in, exploding into action to release some of her pent-up feelings. She stalked up and down the carpet, her hands flying out to emphasise her excuse. 'You saw him, Ray. The way he stared at me. As if I were some new kind of specimen that had to be categorised. And then he flirted . . . flirted!' Her voice rose several decibels. 'You heard what he said. He had no right to flirt with me. He's been courting Jocelyn. My very own sister. It was downright disgusting of him to try that kind of turn-on with me. That man is heartless, Ray. All brain, no feeling. He's going to bring Jocelyn nothing but grief!'

'Antonia . . .' It was a heavy sigh. 'I stared at you too. Whenever you make an entrance people stare at you. You're like . . .' he cast around helplessly for words to describe the startling force of nature that she somehow encapsulated, then gave her a lop-sided smile 'like a supernova bursting through the universe, displacing everything else. In vivid Technicolor.'

The straight eyebrows formed a V of emphatic displeasure. 'I don't mean to be.'

'Antonia, you simply are,' Ray explained patiently. 'When I married your mother and you came into this household, it was like suddenly acquiring a live-in tornado. And there's never been a dull moment since. That's no criticism of you, my dear. I wouldn't like to see you any other way. You've brightened our lives immeasurably. All I'm really saying is that Noah Seton reacted to you as any other man would.'

'What about his supposed attachment to Jocelyn?' Toni protested. No matter how Ray explained it, she had felt signals coming from Noah Seton that weren't right. Not if everything was the way it should be between him and Jocelyn.

'I have no doubt that Noah finds Jocelyn very attractive. In a different way. Initial impact is one thing. Whether one follows it up is something else again. Let me remind you that you control that, Antonia. The woman always does. But it is ungracious to be heavy-handed about it.'

Toni grimaced a partial surrender. 'I'll try to remain polite. But I don't like him, Ray. It's no use saying I do.'

'You haven't given him much of a chance, Antonia,' Ray reminded her with mild irony.

Noah Seton hadn't given a lot of people much of a chance, Toni silently argued. 'I don't see how you can say "in vivid Technicolor" when I'm wearing black!' she said out loud, still deeply affronted by the way Noah Seton had acted towards her.

Ray Clifford viewed her with indulgent amusement. He could almost see sparks flying from her, and it had nothing to do with the colour of her dress. It never would have. 'There is a touch of violet and green,' he pointed out. 'And while we're on the subject of dress, Antonia, we must have a talk about charge accounts soon. Now that I'm retired, there won't be the same cash flow we've had in the past. I don't mean to stint you, but perhaps a little less extravagance could be in order.'

Toni flushed with guilty shame. She hadn't even looked at the price-tag of this dress when she had bought it, but she was wretchedly aware that the boutique at Double Bay didn't stock anything much under seven hundred dollars. And then there were the high-fashion shoes on her feet...

All these years she had dashed off a signature for oodles of expensive clothes without giving it a second thought, as if it were all hers by right, while other people struggled just to survive from pay-cheque to pay-cheque. What she was wearing tonight could probably keep poor old Mr Templeton for a month.

The green eyes lifted to her stepfather were filled with pained apology. 'I'm sorry, Ray. I've taken everything you've given me so much for granted. And I should be keeping myself now. I should have——'

'Antonia....' He shook his head as he took the few paces to reach her and curl his hands around her shoulders. She was such an unpredictable creature, full of wild extremes and passionate feelings erupting in so many different directions that he had never been able to keep up with any of them. But he would not have her any other way. 'Don't take what I said so much to heart, my dear. I love to see you all dressed up in whatever finery you choose.'

He wasn't reaching her. He could sense the turbulent emotions which overrode his words. He lifted one hand and stroked her flushed cheek with tender concern. 'Antonia, it is my pleasure to keep you in the best manner I can. Don't deprive me of that. And now don't make me feel I've spoiled this party for you. It is also my pleasure to see you enjoying yourself. Come, my dear. Smile for me.'

She smiled, her heart overflowing with a burst of love for this man who had been a father to her ever since she was ten years old. His hair was white now, the blue eyes not so bright as they used to be, his handsome face grown heavy with the years, but his kindness to her had never waned, however much of a trial she'd been to him at times. She threw her arms around his rather portly waist and gave him a fierce hug.

'I promise I'll be more considerate in the future, Ray,' she cried fervently.

'That could be very dull,' he replied with an affectionate chuckle. 'But somehow I don't think it will be.'

She lifted rueful eyes. 'I don't know how you've put up with me.'

He tweaked her curls. 'Somewhere along the line it got addictive. And we'd better get moving if this party can't begin without you.'

Toni made a scoffing noise which Ray ignored. He tucked her arm firmly around his and escorted her to the reception-room. Their entrance caused an immediate stir among the crowd of guests. Ray smiled to himself as he felt the wave of anticipation, the charge of raised excitement. Toni was swept from his side to form the nucleus of a suddenly animated group of people. The party was about to start swinging.

Noah Seton's eyes had fastened on Toni the moment she stepped through the doorway. She had felt them, been drawn to them, and was now defying their magnetic pull on her, effervescing with almost manic energy to everyone in her immediate vicinity.

She would get to him before this party ended, she determined. Then she would give him everything she had planned! It was very clear to her that neither Ray nor Jocelyn understood what kind of man they were dealing with. It was well past time that Noah Seton was faced with the truth about himself!

And from across the room Noah Seton watched her, silently determined that before this night was over he would get to her. He could not forget the super-spiked electrical charge that had jolted his body when he first saw her. Nor could he forget her antagonism towards him. Obviously some things needed to be put right.

He vaguely wondered if all his plans and schemes might suddenly be going astray. The thought was tossed aside with a mocking smile. No, he knew precisely where he was heading. He had spent the first part of his life on building a fortune that could virtually multiply by its own weight. He now needed a suitable companion to share the rest of it.

Jocelyn Clifford could make him the right kind of wife. She would give him the right kind of children. And he was ready to do the right thing by her in return. Marriage was just the same as a business, and he had calculated the profit and loss. With Jocelyn the balance was tilted to an acceptable level. Controlled judgement was always the key to success.

In the meantime, it was necessary to administer to that pert little dynamo a very chastening lesson. One thing he didn't need was a problem with Jocelyn's stepsister. He would certainly get to *Miss Braden* before this party ended.

CHAPTER TWO

TONI was not enjoying herself. She worked very hard at appearing to do so, and certainly no one questioned her performance. Her frenetic gaiety seemed infectious to everyone who came in contact with her. Conversation bubbled with wild wit. She danced up a storm that swept everyone up and raged through every room, right out to the back patio. She was, to all intents and purposes, in scintillating party form.

Only she knew how conscious she was of Noah Seton's presence, of those dark eyes continually finding her, boring into her, infuriating her more and more with their probing intensity. He played the part of attentive suitor to her stepsister with a suave sophistication that would have been admirable if Toni didn't know better. He didn't have his mind or heart in that role. He was watching *her*. Waiting—as she was waiting—for the right opportunity... although she had no doubt that he had an entirely different purpose from hers.

Eventually a sumptuous buffet supper was laid on by the catering people. Toni was not hungry. Her insides were churning far too much to appreciate the various delicacies that were urged on her by friends who were eager to tempt her appetite. She nibbled some smoked salmon and sipped champagne for form's sake while she surreptitiously watched Noah Seton.

He mixed effortlessly. Toni couldn't help admiring the way he could gather a group of people around himself and keep them all entertained. As much as she might resent it, there was no denying his personal magnetism.

He did not stay continually with Jocelyn. On the other hand, he did not approach Toni either. It almost seemed to Toni that he was creating an effect. Every move was superbly calculated. Still, she imagined she had a surprise or two in store for him.

Her mind was fermenting with a number of alternative ideas when she was approached by Lillian Devereux, one of the dearest friends her mother had had in the decade or so before she died. Just the sight of Lillian gave Toni a sharp twinge of loss. It had been six years now, but she still missed her mother. She probably always would.

'Toni, may I catch you for a minute?' Lillian appealed with all the charm that had made successful appeals for many worthwhile causes.

Unlike many women who sat on charity committees for the social éclat rather than any real sense of caring, Lillian Devereux genuinely wanted to help those in need, particularly the physically handicapped. She was a diabetic herself, and not in the best of health, but she was still prepared to work tirelessly for those less fortunate.

'Of course, Mrs Devereux,' Toni complied, forcing herself out of her preoccupation with Noah Seton, and throwing a gaily dismissive smile to her companions as she moved forward to take the woman's outstretched hands. She squeezed them gently in affectionate greeting. 'I do like that pinky mauve shade you've put through your hair. It's very feminine and flattering.' And, in truth, Lillian really did look quite lovely dressed in a floating pink and mauve dress that played down her plumpness and toned with her new hairdo.

A hand instantly lifted to primp the soft waves. Her smile beamed with pleasure. 'I'm so glad you think so. I really needed a lift. Things have gone from bad to worse. My cook has left me and I'm having terrible trouble replacing her. But that's not what I meant to talk to you about. You can't cook. But what we have to do... Toni, we simply have to raise money for the deaf children. You must have heard about those wonderful new bionic ear implants?'

'Jocelyn was telling me about them,' Toni acquiesced. She had a sinking feeling about what was coming. Her stepsister spent three days a week at the Camperdown Children's Hospital working on an art-therapy programme for the chronically ill patients. Somehow Toni never had the time available to do these things on a permanent basis, but Mrs Devereux had found a way of using her talents that took up a prodigious amount of time.

'Just think... little children who have never heard before. It's a marvellous thing. But every implant costs more than fifteen thousand dollars. And then there's all the post-operative work, teaching them the skills of hearing, comprehending sounds and speaking... all the things most children have learnt naturally. There's no subsidy from the State Government for it either,' Lillian explained earnestly. 'I think we should aim for a million dollars, Toni.'

'Never aim too low,' Toni quickly agreed, feeling restive under what looked like becoming a long-winded one-minute chat.

'The theme you suggested for the Blind Society Ball last year dragged everybody in. We need a big event, Toni. And you're so good at ideas. I just know you'll be able to come up with something so original and exciting that people will open their pockets as they've never been opened before.'

The expectant sparkle in Lillian Devereux's soft brown eyes really put Toni on the spot. She had so much else on her mind, so much more pressing business that had to be urgently dealt with. Like opening Noah Seton's pocket! And his cold computer mind!

'Let me think about it, Mrs Devereux,' she procrastinated. The ball last year had been fun. Every charity do she had ever suggested had been fun. But Toni wasn't in a fun mood tonight. She forced a reassuring smile. 'If I come up with something, I'll let you know.'

'Please do think about it, Toni,' the older woman pressed. 'Such a worthwhile cause. My little grandniece, Emily...she is one of the ones...' Her voice trailed off, her private distress plain on her face.

Toni resolved to put her mind to it as soon as she had the time. She knew how much she'd hate to be in a soundless world. For one thing, it would deprive her of the opportunity to give Noah Seton the telling off he deserved!

Out of the corner of her eye she saw her stepsister talking to him, then giving his arm a quick squeeze and moving away. Heading towards the powder-room, Toni figured. Jocelyn had an obsession about repairing her make-up after she had eaten. Inspiration leapt to Toni's tongue.

'Have you talked to Jocelyn about it, Mrs Devereux? You'll need to get her in on this. I'm sure she would be interested. She works miracles with children—any children at all. Why don't you have a chat to her while you're here? She might be able to come up with some suggestions.'

'Yes. I'll bring Jocelyn in on it too,' she said with bright enthusiasm, her eyes instantly darting around the crowd for her next quarry. 'If you'll excuse me, Toni...'

The moment her back was turned Toni swung towards Noah Seton. Their eyes clashed, a mutuality of purpose blazing between them. Almost at the same instant he started his move towards her, collecting a glass of champagne from a waiter's tray on the way. He brought it to her, an obvious offering since he already had one in his other hand.

'All these hours of chatting, Miss Braden. Undoubtedly you must feel quite dry,' he drawled lightly, projecting an easy charm that didn't fool Toni for one second. The black eyes were watching, weighing, collecting knowledge.

'How *thoughtful* of you, Mr Seton,' she replied icily.

He had a good poker face. There was not the minutest reaction to her subtle taunt. 'Perhaps I should call you Mrs Sheldon,' he rolled out blandly. 'Would you be more comfortable with that?'

Toni made a mental note to tell Jocelyn she should not talk freely about her to the enemy. Only she couldn't use the word 'enemy'. That would be in bad taste, considering Jocelyn's present inclinations.

'I am no longer married,' she stated, just as blandly.

'It didn't work out?' he asked, injecting a note of sympathetic interest.

'That is a masterpiece of understatement. The idea of marriage is fine. It's what happens afterwards that's the problem.' Her eyes stabbed home the point. He wouldn't make Jocelyn happy. Toni could feel it in her bones. 'Perhaps it's something you should take into consideration, Mr Seton.'

'It must have been really bad,' he concluded. His mouth took on a sardonic little curl. 'Undoubtedly it was all his fault.'

'That's personal!' Toni snapped.

The sharpness in his riveting dark eyes seemed to intensify. 'You don't like me for some reason.'

Toni's mouth curled. 'That's another masterpiece of understatement.'

'What precisely do you feel?'

Her chin lifted in defiance of any pretence to politeness. 'Hate is a fair approximation.'

He didn't even flinch. 'Tell me why.'

'If I do it here, Mr Seton, I might explode.' The green eyes blazed the high probability of that, and her voice could have cut steel as she explained her restraint. 'Not that I mind making a scene. You deserve one. A big one. But, unlike you, I do consider other people, and I don't wish to upset either Jocelyn or Ray.'

He smiled, like a crocodile about to feed well. 'My sentiments exactly. Perhaps the rose-garden?'

A warning tingle crawled down Toni's spine. He was dangerous. Men like him should be put in a cage marked 'Don't Feed the Animals'. Nevertheless, the rose-garden would still be relatively private at this early hour. Later on might be a different matter, but right now it should suit her purpose. Wilfully intent on taking a piece out of him, Toni ignored the danger signals her body was registering. Noah Seton couldn't do anything to her. She wouldn't let him!

Her smile outshone any of Lucrezia Borgia's. 'My own choice exactly! It will give me much pleasure to show you the blood-red blooms of Alamein, the best of Mr Lincoln, and the fine division in colour of York and Lancaster.'

The rose-garden had been her mother's pride and joy, and there wasn't one bush she hadn't identified to Toni a thousand times. It gave Toni an intensely personal satisfaction to name the roses which signified the kind of conflict she had in store for Noah Seton.

His eyes returned a glittering challenge. 'I have a partiality towards Double Delight myself.' Then, while Toni was still startled that he should know the name of any rose, he slid his arm around her waist and smoothly turned her towards the opened doors which led on to the back patio. 'I suggest we go now.'

'Don't you dare touch me!' she hissed at him, sizzlingly aware of the hand resting on the curve of her hip. 'Anywhere!' she added emphatically when the hand slid back to her arm.

One black eyebrow kicked higher as he took in the furious sparks in her eyes. 'It's that serious?'

'Yes,' she bit out through clenched teeth. His 'Double Delight' comment was just sinking in, giving rise to a lot of connotations that didn't bear thinking about. She felt extremely hot and bothered, but still determined to get the better of him.

He dropped his hand and they walked together, in apparently friendly accord, towards the agreed-upon confrontation. No one attempted to interrupt their progress through the crowd. In fact, a clear path opened up for them. Quite simply the innate power of both their personalities—now joined in mutual purpose—intimidated any competition for their separate attention. They left the party behind them without a question being asked.

As the brightness of the lights from the patio diminished, and the shadows of the rose-garden grew darker, Toni became more and more aware of the man at her side. Reluctantly and bitterly she acknowledged what her body had been signalling all night. There was a strong sexual attraction between them. But her marriage had put that particular problem in its proper perspective. Sex was a fine natural thing between a man and a woman. Occasionally it was necessary in order to be normal, but, apart from that, it was only a distraction from real issues. Nevertheless, the distraction was rather disturbing . . . out here in the night . . . alone with him.

'Why don't you admit that the reason for your hostility is simply that you feel threatened by me?'

He slid the question out in a mild tone that nevertheless sliced straight under Toni's skin. She came to a dead halt and glared at him in incredulous scorn. 'In what way do you imagine you threaten me, Mr Seton?'

He faced her with all the arrogant confidence in the world. 'You're attracted to me, and you don't like it. Either because of some hangover from your marriage, or because it makes you feel disloyal towards your stepsister, or a combination of both. Hate is a defence against something you can't control.'

'How wrong you are!' she scoffed, contemptuously dismissing his argument. 'Hate is inspired by actions. Your actions, Mr Seton. And I hated you before I ever laid eyes on you. And not for the psychological claptrap that you've just spouted!'

'Then please enlighten me.' His mouth quirked. 'You look even more intensely beautiful when you're totally furious. It makes you come alive with a vi-

brancy and colour that outshines all the roses. A
spotlight of brilliant energy.'

'You're not taking this seriously!' she accused,
frustrated by his manner and upset by the compliments which she found decidedly improper, considering his relationship with Jocelyn.

His hand lifted and stroked softly down her burning
cheek. 'Is there some reason why I should?' he asked,
his voice a low caress that increased her inner
turbulence.

Toni bit her lip. When she had projected this
meeting in her mind she had imagined a lot of things,
but not that Noah Seton wouldn't take her seriously.
And that touch on her cheek . . . tingling through
her . . . his closeness so disturbing in the soft cocoon
of the night. She stepped back a half-pace, re-
emphasising her rejection of any physical contact with
him and establishing a distance that her eyes
reinforced.

The realisation came that there was no point in
throwing threats at Noah Seton, as she had intended
to do. She was sure now that he would just laugh at
her. She would have to implement them. He couldn't
laugh at action. So she had to go ahead and dem-
onstrate what he should have done by doing it herself.

She had reached a watershed in her life, a point of
no return. It had happened before . . . when her mother
had died . . . when her marriage had ended . . . and this
was another time when she had to take stock and make
another decisive turn. The fierce anger bubbling inside
her subsided, to be replaced by iron determination.
Noah Seton would pay dearly for this.

And one thing could be settled right now. He had
given her the opening to test what he really felt for
Jocelyn. Although there was probably nothing she

could do about it, Toni wanted to know if her judgement was correct.

'You should not be looking at other women,' she began tersely. 'You should not be attracted——'

'Until such time as I marry, I'll look at whomsoever I please,' he returned equably. 'As yet I've made no commitment to your stepsister. Nor she to me. I'm in a position where I have the choice of many roses, Miss Braden. It would not augur well for future harmony to choose one whose loveliness is diminished by an attachment of prickly thorns.'

He paused to let that sink in before pointedly adding, 'I see your irrational antagonism towards me as a serious impediment in any relationship with you . . . or Jocelyn. I want to sort it out.'

Cold and calculating, Toni affirmed. No flame of love or passion would ever sway his judgement. He only cared about what suited him. Never mind what Jocelyn might feel! And the arrogance of the man, to think he could have any woman he chose! Toni hoped that Jocelyn had the good sense to throw him out of her life and shut the door in his face.

Her hands automatically came up to rest on her hips. It was a pose that anyone who knew her would have recognised as trouble with a capital T. It reinforced the determination on her face. 'The feelings I have are anything but irrational, Mr Seton. As you are about to find out.'

She was totally unaware that the paleness of her hands on the black dress picked out the tininess of her waist and the sumptuous curve of her hips. Noah Seton forced his eyes up to hers. 'Fine! I'll just put my hands away so I won't be tempted to offend you again,' he drawled, placing them behind his back in a deliberately patient fashion that was meant to offend.

Somehow the action drew attention to the rest of him. For a moment, Toni lost her grip on all the ideas that had been bursting through her head. Noah Seton was overpoweringly masculine. It stirred something in her that threatened the normal clarity of her thinking. She had to make a concentrated effort to drag Mr Templeton back to the forefront of her mind. He, and the others like him who had lost their jobs, were worth fighting for.

'Now, tell me what this is all about,' Noah Seton invited in the kind of tone one would use with a recalcitrant child.

It helped Toni concentrate her mind wonderfully. Her thoughts meshed into a burning bolt of anger. 'How many people were fired after you completed this take-over?' she shot at him.

Surprise flitted over his face, but he replied with slow, measured consideration. 'I'm not sure. I have people who look after that side of our operations. I suppose twenty or thirty. That would be normal for a company of this size.'

Toni's indignation rose to full flood. 'You just don't care, do you? They're nothing but numbers to you. Not people with needs and wants and feelings——'

'When I take over a company, Miss Braden,' he cut in with cool precision, 'I aim to run it more successfully than was done before. I have a responsibility to my shareholders to do that. Whatever is necessary to achieve that purpose is done. Like surgery, some things are painful. You've got to cut away the dead wood in the operation——'

'How would you like to be considered dead wood?' Toni blasted back at him. 'I'll bet you wouldn't like it. Cut adrift like unwanted flotsam and jetsam! You wouldn't like it one bit. Not one bit more than the people you've done it to. Not if you had any feelings at all.'

His mouth thinned as if he had to make an effort to hold himself in. 'Why don't you tell me your problem? I'll see what can be done about it.'

A sense of triumph boosted Toni's fiery indignation. 'There are twenty-seven people who haven't got a job because of you. You didn't know that. Not precisely. And you didn't know them. Not as individuals——'

'Then there are twenty-seven individuals who have replaced those people,' he returned coolly. 'They've got the jobs. What do you propose? Do you want me to fire efficient executives and replace them with the old staff? How am I supposed to justify that?'

Toni's triumph crashed into frustration. 'Why did you fire our people in the first place? They're not dead wood! They're good, reliable workers. They've been with us for years. Every one of them. You couldn't get any more loyal and dedicated workers than Mr Templeton and——'

'Who is Mr Templeton?'

'See! You don't even know them! You never even looked to find out what you were doing. You're gobbling up other people's lives and——'

'Now just hold on a minute!' he rapped out. His arms whipped out from behind his back and grabbed her shoulders.

Toni forgot what she was saying. Suddenly there was something very formidable and threatening about the breadth of his chest. And somehow he seemed to have grown taller, the hard planes of his face harder. The way his hands squeezed into her flesh didn't help to slow her pulse-rate either. Her heart was thumping madly against the constriction of her chest.

'I do not run a charity,' he said, clipping each word out with biting control. 'I run a business. And a business will die if it's not changed over the years. Grow or die. There is no other way. Your stepfather ran his company as an old family business, and it does not meet the needs of a modern transport network. It was dying on its feet. Moribund! We have to computerise the office-work, change schedules, expand and vitalise. That means staffing changes whether you like it or not, Miss Braden. We've kept all the drivers——'

'You could have tried retraining our people!' she shot at him in fierce rebuttal. 'You didn't have to take their jobs!'

'It's standard practice. Retraining takes time! With no guarantee that they have the capability of being retrained!' he retorted with savage impatience. His fingers dug deeper as if he wanted to shake her. 'Be reasonable!'

'It's so easy for you to say that, isn't it?' she seethed. 'It's not your livelihood being threatened. You're safe and secure up on your pinnacle!'

'And so are you! You've still got your job. Always will. And I'll be delighted to have you working for us——'

'Well, that's one delight you won't have because I haven't got a job with you! And you can get your hands off my person altogether, Noah Seton! Right now!'

His eyes glittered down at her for long, tense seconds. Toni had the forceful impression that he was in two minds as to whether to throttle her or kiss her. Violence shimmered in the small space between them, knotting her nerves and making her pulse run riot. When he finally complied with her demand, he walked away from her for a few paces.

Toni gulped in a few much-needed breaths of clear air. There was an awful fluttery weakness in her stomach. She hastily revised her opinion about Noah Seton's having no feelings. But no way in the world was she going to let him intimidate her. In fact, it gave her a secret sense of triumph to know that she had rocked his control. When he swung around to take up their conversation again, his face was wiped clear of any betraying expression of his thoughts, but Toni noticed that his hands were tightly clenched.

'It was specifically written into the agreement by Ray that you would be retained by the company, Miss Braden,' he stated evenly. 'I always make a point of honouring agreements.'

Her chin came up in proud defiance. 'Ray misunderstood my position on the matter. He thought the job was enough for me. What I actually wanted was to run the company when he retired. And I could have done it, too. But I couldn't convince him that I would never marry again. He's got these old-fashioned ideas——'

'So at last we come to the crux of your hostility!' Noah Seton said with grim satisfaction. '*I've* got what *you* wanted.'

Her eyes flashed her scorn for his conclusion. 'Wrong again! Ray got what he wanted, and that was what was important. I've got personal regrets that he didn't want to trust the company to me, but that is his business and fair enough. The crux of my hostility, Mr Seton, is what *you* are doing to *our* people!' she asserted vehemently.

He frowned, obviously not liking to have his judgement flouted. 'That really concerns you?' he tested.

'Yes! I'll make my own way regardless of what happens! As for my job with *your* company, I've resigned. There's no way I'd work for you. In point of fact, I was only waiting until Monday to do it more effectively.'

'What did you have in mind?' he asked sharply.

She glared at him. 'Do you tell people what you're going to do when you plan a take-over?'

'No.'

'Then I'm not telling you what I'm going to do. One thing only is certain. I've got to do something for all those people that you've dumped on the scrapheap. And you're going to pay for what you've done. I've got friends in high places. One way or another you'll find out what it's like to get hurt.'

His chest expanded as he drew in a deep breath. The tightly clenched fingers uncurled and he lifted one hand in an open gesture of appeasement. 'Look at it this way,' he invited, pitching his tone to pleasant persuasion. 'This is all unnecessary. We're going to expand the present business of this transport company. We'll be creating jobs.'

'That's no consolation to the people who haven't got one now because of you,' she retorted obdurately.

His hand sliced an impatient dismissal. 'I can't be responsible for everyone. In this society some people are winners and some people are losers. In this case, there are going to be far more winners than losers.'

'Well, I'm on the side of the losers! I'm fighting for them. And their rights. The trouble with you is that you're just a computer that makes decisions according to——'

'Miss Braden, enough is enough!' he cut in, his tone one of studied weariness. 'Give it away. Let's settle this matter in a civilised manner. You can't win——'

'I didn't say I was going to win,' she retorted fiercely. 'I said I was going to fight on.'

'Better to deal . . . if you have any bargaining sense at all,' he retaliated.

Toni shut her mouth. She didn't trust him—not after all she had learned about him—but if he was prepared to make concessions, she was not about to jeopardise any hope for other people until she found out what he intended.

He spread both hands in conciliatory appeal. 'I want us to be friends . . .'

'Mr Seton, I can read you like a book,' she said with arch scepticism. 'You want it to be easy.'

He regarded her silently for several moments and there was a knowingness in his eyes that Toni found intensely discomfiting. Then his gaze roved slowly down to her feet and up again, as if taking a detailed inventory of all that she was. A faint self-mocking smile curled his mouth.

'I find you a very disturbing element in my life,' he said, as though he was surprised by the fact.

Toni was still burning from having been subjected to the insolence of his appraisal. 'By the time I've finished you'll be a lot more disturbed, I can assure you of that,' she said heatedly.

'I'll be at the company offices on Monday. Come to me then and we'll talk about what can be done.'

Toni seethed at his casual assumption of control. She was not about to go to him as some supplicant. That wasn't the way to bargain. 'You come to me on Monday and tell me what you can do,' she retorted.

His eyes narrowed. 'You won't resign, Miss Braden.'

'I have resigned. I'll only be going in to finish up a few things.'

'You're a very implacable young woman.'

'You're a monster of a man.'

His face broke into a grin that totally disarmed Toni. She was jolted by a sudden and sharp appreciation of what Jocelyn saw in him. The magnetic intelligence of those disturbing dark eyes was nothing to the mesmerising charm of that grin. It was positively indecent, considering the soulless nature of the man.

'You've made your position clear. Now, let's leave it until Monday,' he said with a most unsettling throb of anticipation in his voice. 'Meanwhile, the night is still young and you haven't shown me the roses you promised me. Please lead on.'

Toni was gripped by a sense of uncertainty that was totally foreign to her. Noah Seton was right. She had said all she meant to say at this point. However, every instinct told her it was dangerous to stay with him, out here in the rose-garden. On the other hand, to retreat felt equally wrong. He was throwing out a challenge that had to be met if she was to prove herself an adversary to be reckoned with.

Deeply suspicious of his motives, but determined to play the pretence out, Toni strolled forward casually and began identifying the roses on either side of them as they continued around the path. Noah Seton made appreciative comments that she couldn't take exception to, but his eyes sparkled with some secret amusement that told Toni better than words that he intended manipulating this scene to his advantage. Or her disadvantage. Computer was too good a name for him. He was a cold, calculating devil! And that quick grin he had was the wickedest thing in his armoury!

It was more of a relief than an embarrassment to Toni when they came face to face with Jocelyn emerging from the trellised walkway that supported all the climbing roses. She was arm in arm with another man, and Toni instantly seized the opportunity to part with Noah Seton.

Ignoring the shadow of dismay that flitted over Jocelyn's face at the sight of them together, Toni brightly demanded an introduction to her stepsister's companion, took charge of him herself with a burst of gay chatter, then swept him back to the party, leaving Jocelyn with the blithe admonition to continue indulging Noah Seton's fascination with the rose-garden.

The strong sense of those black eyes boring into her back made Toni bubble with elation. She had foiled Noah Seton's game—whatever it was—and when next they met she would be more than ready for anything he might do or say. She would make Monday a red-letter day in his life's diary! He certainly wouldn't be grinning when she'd finished taking him apart. And there would be no amusement left in his eyes either!

CHAPTER THREE

As TONI steered Jocelyn's erstwhile escort back to the party, she silently vowed that she would not look at Noah Seton again tonight. She would not give him that satisfaction. He might be a sexy male animal, but she was not attracted to him in anything other than a physical sense—which was inconvenient and unfortunate—and she would give him absolutely nothing on which to feed his monumental ego.

Tomorrow she would begin organising *events*. There was no doubt now that threats against Noah Seton were hopelessly idle. She would have to proceed with more concrete plans. On Monday she could...

'Just who the hell do you think you are?'

Toni looked up at her hijacked companion in startled surprise. Clearly he was put out for some reason, and she instantly set about lifting his spirits again, her reply bubbling with the exhilaration of the moment, her eyes inviting a return to good humour, her mouth teasing with laughter.

'I'm the thorn upon the rose...the joker in the pack...the cat among the pigeons...the phantom of the opera... Oh, a lot of wonderful things I never realised before!'

He didn't smile. But a sense of power zinged through Toni's veins as she began to comprehend the leverage Noah Seton had given her by admitting he wanted to be friends with her. He would have to do a lot of earning to get that friendship! Maybe that was what he'd been trying to do in the garden—

playing at *being nice*! As if she would be fooled by that!

However, that was not the present issue. Richard—she couldn't recall his surname—was not only un-smiling, he was grimly unamused. He was actually looking balefully at her. It hardened the sensitive lines of his handsome face and sharpened the vivid blue of his eyes. He was very good-looking, although Toni didn't particularly go for men with blond hair.

'That was a fair description of yourself until you got to the phantom of the opera,' he said caustically. 'I found *him* a sympathetic character.'

Obviously Richard felt no sympathy with her. 'Is something wrong?' Toni asked, doing her best to sober her wayward thoughts and concentrate on the problem. Clearly she had offended him. Badly.

'Yes! Thanks to you and your uninvited inter-ference!' he said acidly. 'Until you came along every-thing was all right. I was in the rose-garden. I was with Jocelyn——'

'I'm sorry——'

'So you should be!' he snapped, his eyes glinting with angry frustration. 'In future, would you be kind enough to stay with the companion of your choice?'

'I said I'm sorry,' Toni repeated earnestly. 'But the truth of the matter is that Noah Seton is not my choice of companion, and all I did was bring him and Jocelyn together to get on with their real business.'

He frowned. 'What business?'

Toni sighed. 'The usual business between an ex-tremely eligible man and a woman. Jocelyn has every-thing to recommend her as a future wife.'

'Marriage?' He sounded appalled.

'Well, it's not certain yet.' Toni sincerely hoped it never would be.

Richard breathed a vicious curse. His gaze lifted and swept around the huge high-ceilinged room with all its elegant furnishings. His finely moulded mouth thinned into a grim line as his focus lowered to pick over the expensively dressed guests. 'I shouldn't have come here. I should have known better,' he muttered. Then, without another word or even a last glance at Toni, he pushed off through the crowd, driven determination in every step.

Toni stared after him. He was clearly a very intense young man. I must talk to Jocelyn about him, she thought. Then a couple of wild revellers pounced on her and carried her off to join in the dancing, and Toni postponed any more serious thinking until after the party was over.

She kept to her resolution not to look at Noah Seton again, although she was aware of when precisely he returned from the rose-garden with Jocelyn. The atmosphere of the party somehow heightened at his re-entrance. She was also aware of those watchful dark eyes resting on her from time to time. It made her feel more vividly alive than she had ever felt in her life. What she had always needed, Toni decided, was a challenge worthy of her mettle. The party ended up being more fun than she had ever imagined.

It was only after everyone had gone and she was alone in her bedroom that Toni really began to get her mind in order and focused on what had to be done. A re-employment service was clearly indicated. She had plenty of good contacts and she could give glowing references. There was no reason why she couldn't find good jobs for every one of those twenty-seven people.

But first she would need an office. She could hardly operate from the company building once she had left it. And she couldn't use Ray's home for business calls. That wasn't fair. Retirement was retirement, and she was going to be much more considerate to Ray's needs from now on. So she had to get an office of her own.

Which brought her to money! She wondered how much it cost to rent an office in the city. And how much the initial outlay might be. Once she got her re-employment business running, she would earn commissions that should cover costs, but until then... money was a problem.

There was a time when Toni had had quite a lot of money in her own right, but Murray Sheldon had divested her of the inheritance from her mother. Of course, that was her own fault. She had been mad to marry him, mad to trust him. Which just went to show how blinded one could be by sexual attraction. Well, she had learnt that lesson, and at the time she hadn't cared how much it had cost her. It was worth it, just to be out of that stupid marriage.

What little she had left had somehow disappeared over the years. She was never quite sure how it went, but then she had never gone without anything she *really needed*. It was the same with her income from work. She gave it away, lent it to friends, spent it on things. She simply wasn't very good at sticking to money. It was a commodity to be used for whatever seemed like a good idea at the time. She hadn't realised until these last few weeks just how fortunate she was to have the fall-back security of a good home where the door was always open for her. And Ray to cosset and spoil her.

It was well past time she stood on her own two feet and proved herself capable of it. Which Toni didn't doubt for a second. She would not ask Ray for a loan. She would raise the money for the office by herself.

She could always hock her pearls if she had to. Or sell some of her clothes to a second-hand shop. There was always a way to do anything. And she would find it.

'Toni?' Jocelyn's voice whispered around the bedroom door. 'Are you still awake?'

'Wide awake! Come on in,' Toni promptly invited, leaning over to switch on the bedside lamp.

Jocelyn looked wonderfully ethereal in a floating white nightie and négligé. Toni herself was wearing a cotton nightshirt with a Kermit-the-frog motif, which had appealed to her sense of humour. Maybe some day some frog of a man might turn into a prince worth sharing her bed and life with. It was a fantasy that Toni had extreme doubts about, but she was not one to give up on dreams. Not entirely anyway.

Toni thought again how very beautiful her step-sister was. However, the smile on Jocelyn's face seemed a trifle over-bright for this time of night—or late pre-dawn, to be more exact.

'I wanted to ask what you thought of Noah now you've met him?' she asked, relaxing across the end of the bed as Toni hitched herself up on the pillows.

'About the same as before I met him,' Toni answered drily. 'But he's certainly a macho hunk of a man, if that's what you want to be told.'

Jocelyn gave a laugh that sounded a bit tinny. 'He's total man all right. He goes after what he wants. Which is more than can be said for some.' Her eyes flickered with uncertainty. 'He asked a lot of questions about you, Toni.'

'Just doing his homework on a prickly sister-in-law. And don't answer any more questions on anything. The less he knows, the better.' Toni threw her a teasing grin to settle any doubts Jocelyn might have in her mind about that meeting in the rose-garden.

'He said you had a talk about the take-over and he's going to look into the problems you raised.' Jocelyn was obviously prompting for more.

'Yes. I did some spadework. Hopefully something might come of it,' Toni answered blandly. 'He must think a lot of you, Jocelyn. I doubt he'd bother otherwise.'

'Oh, I don't know,' Jocelyn sighed, and plucked discontentedly at the bedcover. 'I'm not really sure what he thinks of me. He's very nice . . . very mature and sure of himself . . . gentlemanly . . . but sometimes I think he's too smart. He seems to read my mind . . . know what I am . . . what I want to do. I get the feeling he'll take over my life. And I'm not sure I want that.' Her lovely mouth tilted into a lop-sided smile. 'Am I crazy, Toni?'

'It's your life, Jocelyn. You've got to decide what you want,' Toni answered quietly, wanting to press against the man, but knowing she had no right to interfere.

Jocelyn brooded for several moments. 'I guess I'm crazy. I'd have to be to let him get away.'

'Have you gone to bed with him, Jocelyn?'

The blunt question earned a reproving look. Jocelyn was very private about sexual matters. Toni wondered if she was still a virgin, although she was only a year younger than herself. When no answer was readily forthcoming she shrugged and offered an appeasing smile.

'Well, it's one way of getting to know what you want or don't want. It didn't work for me. But it's the usual thing when two people are thinking of getting married.'

Jocelyn relented. 'One of the things I like about Noah is that he's not all over me like a rash! Not like other men. He's restrained. And what he does, he does...with real sensitivity.' A self-conscious blush stained her cheeks. 'I don't have to go to bed with him to know he'll be a good lover, Toni. He's not pressing me. I like that too!'

'Fine! It just sounds a bit cold-blooded to me,' Toni remarked flippantly, unaccountably disturbed by the idea of Noah Seton's being at all sensitive. 'What makes you so sure he's thinking of marriage?'

'The kind of things he talks about. I know he's serious, Toni.'

Toni thought that what was to happen on Monday and thereafter would be a good gauge of how serious Noah Seton was about her stepsister, but she couldn't tell Jocelyn that. At least, if he changed his mind, she didn't think Jocelyn would be too heart-broken. As she pondered the comments her stepsister had made, another thought slipped into Toni's mind.

'How well do you know that Richard what's-his-name who was in the rose-garden with you?' she asked curiously.

Jocelyn's face went oddly still. 'Richard Gilbert? He's a doctor at Camperdown Hospital. We're just friends. Why do you ask?'

'I think he fancies you. He was mad as a hatter when I hauled him back to the party with me.'

'I didn't hear him protesting at the time,' Jocelyn remarked with a decidedly waspish note in her voice.

'Well, I can tell you one thing. He sure didn't fancy me for doing it. And when I explained that you had a thing going with Noah Seton he wasn't too pleased about that either. You'd better be kind to him,

Jocelyn. He's obviously carrying some kind of torch for you.'

A surprisingly catlike little smile played about Jocelyn's mouth. 'He's only ever been friendly towards me.'

'Well, think again,' Toni advised. 'He was fairly burning tonight. And not with good humour.'

'He's very good with children,' Jocelyn said, warmth turning her eyes golden.

'That's nice,' Toni encouraged.

'Yes,' Jocelyn agreed. Still smiling to herself, she gracefully lifted herself off the bed and wafted towards the door. 'Thanks for making the party go so well, Toni,' she said liltingly. 'Goodnight.'

'Sweet dreams,' Toni returned.

A satisfied smile curved her own lips as she snapped off the light and settled back down on the pillows. If Jocelyn secretly fancied Richard Gilbert, and the young doctor had enough gumption to declare his feelings...

Obviously Jocelyn had been obtuse in her dealings with him. The good doctor had to be actively encouraged. Anything that put a spanner in Noah Seton's works was only to the good. It would be a chastening and beneficial experience for him to find out he couldn't have any woman he chose.

Toni put that item on her mental list of things to be acted on. Which brought her back to Noah Seton.

Human relationships were the very devil! And, on a purely pragmatic level, Toni couldn't deny that Noah Seton had a lot going for him... tall, dark and handsome, as wealthy as Croesus, charm on tap when he chose to use it, and a *sensitive* lover as well!

Toni couldn't help wondering how good he was in that department. It was certainly a temptation. For some reason—which she didn't stop to analyse—she felt relieved that he hadn't taken Jocelyn to bed. No commitment . . . as yet. That was what he had said.

He probably made love like a computer, she thought scornfully. All expertise and no feeling. She wondered if he had coldly calculated Jocelyn's sensitivity rating, just to make sure she would respond to him in the satisfactory manner that he required of a wife. All a very controlled exercise, like everything else.

Except for those very few moments tonight. He had teetered on the edge of losing his cool with her then. Somehow Toni doubted that he would have used any sensitivity at all if he had kissed her at that moment. Not that she had wanted him to, of course, but she wouldn't have minded knowing how he kissed . . . just as an item of information. All knowledge was useful, and it was often very hard to say when it would come in handy.

Toni punched the pillows up and settled herself for sleep. She concentrated on relaxing every muscle in her body from the toes up, and, with the ease of a person whose conscience was perfectly clear, she dropped into peaceful unconsciousness.

Sunday was one of those glorious days when the sky was such an iridescent blue that it hurt to look at it. It was a day made for sailing on Sydney Harbour, or surfing at one of the many beaches that graced the city coastline, or boating down the Hawkesbury River, water-skiing, wind-surfing . . . The temptations danced through Toni's mind as she leaned on her bedroom window-sill and breathed in the marvellous morning.

But there were other people with only gloom ahead of them, and today was the day to start shouldering responsibilities. There was no putting it off. That would only make a mockery of her resolution. An office had to be found and rented. There was business to organise. Today could not be a day of pleasure and rest. That alone would constitute some proof to Noah Seton how serious she was.

Toni dragged herself away from the window and went downstairs for Sunday brunch. The cleaning contractors had already been and gone; the house was restored to its usual pristine state. Jocelyn was apparently not up yet. The live-in housekeeper, Mrs Frobisher, was pouring Ray some coffee as he sat at the breakfast-table with the Sunday newspapers spread out in front of him. Toni greeted both of them, dropped a kiss on Ray's cheek, answered Mrs Frobisher's question about what she wanted to eat, then hunted out the *Sydney Morning Herald* from the pile of old newspapers in the kitchen.

Having armed herself with a biro and the pages which contained the office-to-let advertisements, she sat down at the table opposite Ray and set to work, marking out the best-sounding possibilities for what she wanted.

'Er... what are you doing that for, Antonia?' Ray asked in a puzzled fashion.

'I need an office,' she replied matter-of-factly. 'I'm going to start a business.'

'Whatever for?' he questioned with good humour.

'I'm going to be self-supporting, Ray,' she announced. 'I'm not asking for any help from you or from anyone else.'

'Ah!' he said, and fell into an omniscient silence.

Mrs Frobisher brought her omelette and bacon. Toni thanked her and thought once more that she herself really ought to learn to cook. That had been one of the minor problems in her marriage. On the other hand, since she wasn't going to marry again

there wasn't much point in learning to cook when Mrs
Frobisher did it so well. The omelette was delicious.
With her energy recharged for the task ahead of her,
Toni excused herself from the table, carrying her
homework with her.

'Antonia...' Ray called after her, and gave her a
wry little smile as she turned around. 'Please feel free
to come to me before you get into any deep problems.
With the business, I mean. I know you're a very en-
thusiastic worker, my dear, but you're not really very
good with money.'

'I'm going to learn, Ray,' she said with determination. 'You've got to admit I'm good at learning.'

'That's true,' he admitted, without much conviction. 'Well, good luck with your office-hunting,
Antonia. Let me know how you get on.'

She flashed him a smile for which he would just
about forgive her anything. He weakly returned it.
Never a dull moment, he reminded himself as she went
off on her latest quest. Apparently she was not going
to work for Noah Seton. Which was probably just as
well if Noah was going to marry Jocelyn. One thing
he wasn't going to do was start worrying about it. He
rustled through the newspapers again. Retirement was
wonderful.

Toni examined her wardrobe. She had to look like
a serious businesswoman as well as act like one. She
wasn't about to let some sharp estate agent, like
Murray Sheldon, think he could put anything over on
her. She was certainly going to watch every financial
outlay from now on, and keep account of it—if she
could.

She chose a black and white shirtwaister with black
accessories and was well pleased with the effect: smart,
sexy, but definitely no-nonsense.

Some five hours later Toni straggled home exhausted. She was considerably sobered by some of the harsher realities of life. Especially when you didn't have any money. She had eventually found and talked an agent into letting her rent a dingy little room in a rather depressing area. It was *called* an office. And, despite its air of seediness, it still cost the earth. Only by comparing the rents of a lot of other offices had she reluctantly conceded that what was being demanded was fair enough.

Even so, it had taken a lot of persuasion to get the agent to defer the first fortnight's payment in advance. Her smart choice of dress had helped, she decided, since the agent had kept sizing her up while she talked. Undoubtedly he had mentally assessed the cost of her clothes and her home address and decided to take a chance. The question of a lease had been provisionally deferred. But he had made her sign a document like an IOU until such time as her solicitor could examine the legalities. Toni didn't mind that. She was used to signing for things. She had been doing it all her life.

Perhaps the agent was desperate for a tenant. Any tenant. Anyway, she had somehow convinced him that what she was doing constituted the best day's work he had ever done.

As an office, it would do. She didn't really need to impress anyone with it, since she was the only one who had to work there. All her important contacts would be by telephone. The agent had promised to have that reconnected first thing tomorrow, and he had agreed that she didn't have to pay anything until it was operational.

He had looked a bit dazed by the time she had finished talking to him. But he had returned her parting smile, albeit a little weakly, and Toni was sure he would continue to be a very understanding person. Not at all like her ex-husband.

'Did you find an office, Antonia?' Ray asked over dinner.

'Yes. It's near Central Railway, just off Broadway. Easy for people to come to me,' she explained.

It needn't stay dingy, she thought. She could paint it yellow, a nice hopeful colour for people down on their luck. Maybe a touch of green. Green was very restful for anxious minds. And if she put some interesting motifs on the walls...brought in a couple of lush pot-plants...

'What do you want an office for?' Jocelyn asked.

'Antonia is starting a business,' Ray informed her, while Toni's mind dwelled on that bright inner vision.

'What kind?' Jocelyn persisted, her eyes alight with curiosity.

Toni clicked back to the present. 'It's sort of an employment agency. Re-careering. That kind of thing,' she answered airily. 'I have a few other ideas as well.'

Jocelyn shook her head incredulously. 'Why?'

'Because I want to,' Toni replied.

Which stopped all questions. Both Jocelyn and Ray were well aware that, short of earthquake, fire or cyclone, there was no stopping Toni when she wanted to do something. And, of course, she did not want to go over the matter in any depth, as it could be taken as an implied criticism of Ray's decision to sell the company.

After a short silence while her family pondered where this new move might lead to—which was totally unpredictable anyhow—Toni asked Jocelyn whether she had seen Noah Seton today.

'No. He had some business to see to,' Jocelyn answered distractedly.

It confirmed Toni's opinion that the man had no soul. How else could he have spent such a glorious day on business? It was different for her. Her sense of humanity had necessitated what she had done. But Noah Seton wouldn't have needed to do business. He just couldn't let that computer stop running. She would teach him a thing or two tomorrow.

To ram the first lesson home, Toni did not go to the transport company offices at all on Monday morning. She went straight to her own office, only delaying her arrival there by an hour or so while she requisitioned a fine rhododendron and two splendid hanging cacti—which Ray wouldn't miss at all from the fern-house in the garden—then stopped briefly at a hardware store to pick up several paint colour-charts and a couple of cheap wall-brackets on which to hang the plant baskets.

Her timing was perfect. The Telecom man was actually in her office fixing up the telephone for her, and he had the tools to put up the wall-brackets, which he obligingly did, admiring her choice of plants and wishing her well in her new venture. In fact, he was so keen to be helpful to her that Toni ended up having to usher him out of the office so she could get to work on the telephone.

She got her notebook and biro out of her handbag and started off by ringing the transport company. She spoke to all the retrenched employees who were still working out their notice, telling them where her office was, making appointments for them to come to her, and promising to place them in good jobs as soon as she could. One of the old hands in the trucking division promised to collect her desk and chair—which

Ray had bought especially for her and which certainly didn't belong to Noah Seton—and bring it right over. She finished up this first round of calls with a courteous chat to Noah Seton's secretary, leaving her name, telephone number, and office address should he wish to contact her.

For a short breather from business, she then rang Camperdown Hospital and asked to speak to Dr Richard Gilbert. He turned out to be a pathologist, and in the course of a very interesting conversation with him, during which she dropped a few fertile seeds concerning human relationships, Toni found out quite a few things about pathology that gave her also fruitful pause for thought. Talking to people could be very educational and useful if one was alert enough.

The desk and chair arrived, and Toni really began to feel professional. She took ten minutes off to eat the salad lunch Mrs Frobisher had packed for her, then started ringing a number of people in the transport industry in search of job openings. Each person she spoke to was an individual and had to be treated as such. To some of the executives she could stress loyalty. This was important to them, and she used it to reinforce the value of long-term relationships. If she could remove some of the business from Noah Seton, and place it with the individuals he had sacked . . .

Other executives had to be treated differently. They were looking for efficiency, intimate knowledge of the industry, and a host of other things. Toni saw her job as finding out their needs and then supplying the right person for the job. She jotted down every promising contact, then went further afield, calling every person she could think of who might be helpful, even the gossip columnist, with whom she had a most interesting chat.

Ring, ring, ring ... It was quite exhausting work, but exhilarating too. By late afternoon she had managed to contact all the fired employees who had already left the transport company. Mr Templeton was the last of them, and she had just finished cheering him up when there was a knock on the office door.

'Come in!' she called gaily as she wrote down Mr Templeton's appointment in her notebook. She was immensely pleased that he had agreed to come in tomorrow, despite his pessimism over his prospects. The poor old darling was her biggest challenge!

And then Noah Seton stepped into her office and Toni hastily revised that last thought. The biggest challenge was right here and now, embodied in the man in front of her!

CHAPTER FOUR

NOT for one moment had Noah Seton considered that she would have the power to jolt him a second time. That incredible initial impact was a thing of the past...experienced...gone...unrepeatable! Yet when she looked up at him his irritation and impatience just melted away and he completely forgot what he was supposed to be doing.

He didn't know that Toni had chosen to wear a dazzling scarlet dress as an expression of her intention to make this a red-letter day for him. He didn't know that the brilliant scarlet of the cactus flowers hanging down the window behind her was a purely coincidental colour reflection of her innate vibrancy. He was simply stopped dead in his tracks, struck once again by the unbelievable vitality of the woman in front of him. She rose from the chair behind the desk, and he was hit even more deeply by the sheer force of her feminine sexuality—a force that rattled all his fondly held beliefs that men who allowed themselves to be side-tracked by a transient need for a woman were utter fools.

Toni stood up because she fought better on her feet, because she instinctively used action to lend emphasis to words, and because the look in Noah Seton's eyes stirred her into a restlessness that didn't sit well. She had forgotten how formidable he could be in the flesh, and the dark pin-striped suit he wore gave him an air of dominant masculinity which Toni was ready to defy to her last breath!

After all, she had made him come to her. For the present, she had the upper hand. The inner exultation which rose from this thought brought a glow of pleasure. A sense of delicious mischief quivered on her lips as she pertly asked, 'Is there anything I can do for you, Mr Seton?' She waved towards her one and only chair. 'Would you like to sit down?'

He seemed to give himself a little shake. His gaze flicked to the chair, the desk, then wandered slowly around the grubby puce-coloured walls, dropped to the cracked linoleum floor, and finally returned to her. One satanic eyebrow kicked upwards.

'I thought you would be more smartly fitted out, Miss Braden. Do you call this an office?'

Toni smarted under his condescension. Her chin automatically lifted in a show of lofty unconcern. 'I'm starting at the bottom,' she declared airily. 'I'm making my own way.'

'You certainly are!' he drawled, his mouth curling sardonically.

The green eyes flashed fire, but she managed to project a note of condescension into her own voice. 'Give me time, Mr Seton, and I'll see what I can make of it. In a few days you won't recognise this room. Apart from that, this building is particularly well located. It will eventually become a very important building. Even now I'm looking towards the time when I can buy it.'

To add even more authority to her claim she embroidered a bit. 'Did Jocelyn tell you my ex-husband was in property? I learnt a great deal from him, Mr Seton.' Which was quite true, but the lessons learnt were not exactly in the realm of property. 'I learn a lot from a great many people,' she added for good measure. Then smiled. 'Including you.'

He gave her that quick, punch-to-the-heart grin. 'I'm pleased to be able to help you once again, Miss Braden.'

He strolled forward and casually seated himself on the corner of her desk, one foot planted on the floor, but the other leg swinging quite close to her. Toni couldn't help but notice how the fine cloth of his trousers was stretched tight around a powerfully muscled thigh. Certainly not weedy, she confirmed distractedly. The other consequence of this move was that his eyes were now on the same level as hers, which made it even harder to look away. The magnetic intensity of those brilliant dark eyes was highly disconcerting at close quarters.

'In fact, that's precisely what I've come about,' he said.

Toni frowned, struggling to recollect what he had said before. What was he talking about? Every instinct she had was warning her that this show of charm was strictly a façade, and underneath it was a coiled cobra poised to strike. She had to be wary.

'You *want* to be of service to me, Mr Seton?' Her eyebrows lifted fractionally in disbelief.

Again came that quick grin to disarm her. 'As a reasonable man, I gave consideration to what you said on Saturday night, Miss Braden. There is a certain amount of right in what you propounded. I have gone out of my way to do something about it. I even spent yesterday going over personnel files. I am prepared to satisfy your demands and appease your sense of injustice. I can now find work in my other companies for six of the people who were put off——'

'You can?' Toni couldn't suppress her surprise. She certainly hadn't expected him to take her words so much to heart. Which just went to show she had been right about how unjust he had been in the first place. 'That's a good start,' she said approvingly.

'Now come back to work for me,' he slid out as she was still contemplating just how far she might be able to push him. 'I did promise Ray. I want to live up to that promise.'

A bubble of laughter burst from Toni's throat. 'You thought it would be that easy?' Her eyes danced at him in teasing challenge. 'Oh, no, Mr Seton. I'm delighted that you can place six of my people. And I'll certainly accept those jobs on their behalf. But I'm afraid that doesn't buy my complacency. There are twenty-one losers left and I have to look after them. This is not the end. This is hardly even the beginning of the beginning.'

The charm lost some of its shine. His eyes hardened into black pebbles. 'You can't do something for everyone, Miss Braden.'

'That's probably true,' she agreed. 'But I'm going to try.'

Now that he had shown his hand, Toni's confidence soared to an exhilarating peak. She picked up her notebook from the desk, flicked it open, and, with her pen poised for action, she gave Noah Seton an arch look of enquiry.

'Who are the six? I'll tick them off my list and pass on the good news to them.'

His eyes glittered with some suppressed emotion. Toni suspected it was frustration. 'Without your compliance, perhaps I'll just have to change my mind,' he said softly.

Toni grinned cheekily at him. 'No. *You* won't back down, Mr Seton. Because that would prove I've got a hold on you. People like you would never admit something like that, not even to themselves. You perceive yourself as too much in control of everything and everyone around you to admit any such thing. So I know you won't back down.'

Her eyes clashed fiercely with his, asserting her certainty on this point of charcter. 'Their names, please,' she asked again with absolute confidence.

She saw the glittering pin-points of savage anger burn into his eyes. They flared, receded, simmered with other violent feelings. Toni was forcefully reminded of those moments in the rose-garden when she hadn't known whether he was going to throttle her or sweep her into his arms and kiss her senseless. Her heart had begun to cavort in a most intemperate fashion and her throat was going drier by the second. She couldn't afford to think of how treacherously the rest of her body was reacting to him, because, no matter what was happening or what would happen, she had taken a position from which she would never back down either! It was a matter of principle and pride!

He compressed his lips as if he was clenching his teeth at the same time, then forced enough relaxation to push out words in a slow, precise delivery that bespoke grimly held control.

'Take-overs invariably stir resentments and the destructive type of stubbornness that insists that "the old way" is better than "the new". It's far more efficient to simply clear house and get people who are only too happy to work my way. And, since you persist in being unreasonable——'

Toni used the last resort. She laughed at him. 'But it's not my reasonableness you want, is it, Mr Seton?'

He went very still. Except for his hands. They clenched so tightly that the knuckles shone white.

'What is it that you think I want, Miss Braden?' he asked very quietly.

Toni instantly had the sense of treading a thin, dangerous line. Yet all her knowledge of Noah Seton, to this point, assured her she was on the right track. Her chin tilted in defiant confidence as she tossed his motivation straight in his face.

'You want to be friends with me. God knows why...'

'Friends...' His mouth seemed to curl around the word, mocking it. 'Somehow I don't think we're ever going to be friends, Miss Braden.'

He slowly unfolded himself from the desk, sending a wave of turbulence through Toni as he straightened to his full height again. His gaze held hers with a kind of menacing intensity, and it took all of her innate stubbornness to return a look of steadfast unconcern. She was overwhelmingly aware of his superior physical strength, the aggressive masculinity that emanated from him with heart-squeezing power. It appalled her that he should make her feel so weak-kneed and trembly inside. She might be of small stature in comparison to him, but that didn't mean she was helpless. Far from it.

Nevertheless, it was with considerable relief that she watched him turn aside. He seemed about to walk away, but then he reached out and very deliberately plucked one of the vibrant scarlet flowers from the cactus plant she had hung in front of the window. With a slow sensuality that disturbed Toni anew, he gently rubbed the silky bloom between his fingers. Then, with the same controlled deliberation, he took the couple of steps which brought him close to her, drew the soft petals slowly, shiveringly up the bare skin of her arm, and, as she stood in motionless thrall to his totally unexpected actions, he tucked the flower into the thick black curls above her ear, fixing it in the same way that native Polynesians wore a hibiscus.

Her intuition screamed that the control of this meeting was slipping out of her hands. She had to get it back fast or the victory that had been in her grasp would turn into a loss.

'Why did you do that?' she demanded, her voice little more than a husky breath.

His gaze shifted slowly from the flower to meet hers, and he made no attempt to disguise the glint of self-derision which accompanied his reply. 'It seemed an appropriate way to say goodbye.'

'Giving up, Mr Seton?' she taunted.

'Sometimes the game isn't worth the candle, Miss Braden,' he drawled.

He stared at her for several seconds, then shook his head and walked away from her, laughing softly— even pleasantly—to himself. He moved towards the door and Toni thought he intended to leave.

A tumult of conflicting feelings shot through her, the predominant one being a sharp pang of regret. Which was very confusing, considering the fact that she was sure Jocelyn would be a lot better off without him as her husband.

Then at the last second he wheeled around, the hard lines of his face warring with an odd look of whimsy. 'In future, Miss Braden,' he mocked, 'I think I'll call you Toni. Not because we are friends...'

'Then why?' she asked, unable to grasp what was going on. He had just said goodbye, hadn't he? But now he was talking about the future!

'Because I want you to call me Noah,' he answered, his mouth twitching in some secret amusement.

Toni's confusion increased. What was he suggesting ... if not the friendship he had previously declared he wanted? Wasn't the whole aim of this exercise to smooth his path to a harmonious relationship with Jocelyn's family? And why did she have the feeling he was reassessing her from another angle entirely.

Only one thing was certain. Noah Seton was no push-over. And she had better get her foot on to some gains while she could. Toni took a deep breath to settle the fluttery weakness in her stomach and forced her mind back on to the job.

She flashed him a devastating smile of agreement. 'If that is the case, Mr Seton . . . Noah . . . what are the names of the six people you've chosen to re-employ?'

He reeled off their names without hesitation, almost as if they were irrelevant to what was really going on in his mind. Toni ticked them off her list, pleased that their future looked immeasurably brighter, although there were still twenty-one people who had to be placed somewhere. She closed the notebook with a small sigh of satisfaction, then mentally girded herself to face her adversary once more.

He had leaned back against the door as though he was not about to leave in a hurry. His hands were shoved into his pockets in a deceptively languid pose. Toni, however, was not deceived. There was purpose behind everything Noah Seton did. It was in the nature of the man. He had stayed because he wanted to achieve something with her, and it was up to Toni to milk that for all it was worth.

'You can't squeeze in a few more good workers?' she pressed, more as an opening gambit than with any hope he would go any further down that track.

'As I told you before, Miss Braden, I run a business, not a charity. I've done what I could without displacing other people,' he drawled, confirming her judgement.

'Then there is only one other thing you can do for me,' Toni assured him brightly.

'What?' he asked lazily.

'Venture capital,' she tossed at him. 'I need some. You've got it. I want it.'

His mouth quirked. 'Correct me if I'm wrong, but my understanding of venture capital is money you outlay on some wild scheme that usually loses everything. Like oil wells, gold mines ...'

'Exactly! That's precisely the kind of money I need. And you're in the best possible position to be able to afford it.'

Hard mockery answered her. 'I never expected to be wanted just for my money. But it appears it has its attractions.'

His comment scraped over the raw spot that Murray Sheldon had left on Toni's soul. 'I've been through that too. Not much fun, is it?' she flashed, before pride sealed over the past. 'But we're not bartering love or wants here, are we, Mr Seton? More a matter of righting a wrong.'

'The name I want to hear is Noah ... Toni,' he replied slowly. 'May I ask what you intend doing with this venture capital?'

Toni decided she would allow his first name in return for the venture capital. Simple expedience. An idea had come to her while she had been talking to Dr Richard Gilbert. It needed careful phrasing. She could hardly admit it had come from a man who might very well be trying to steal Jocelyn's affections from Noah Seton.

'I have my own ideas on how this transport business can be developed. They're not in competition with what you're already doing,' she inserted quickly, anxious not to alienate his interest. 'Couriers, to be precise. I need a refrigerated van.'

'What for?' he asked, scepticism threading his voice. 'What do you plan on delivering? Meat . . . ice-cream . . . bodies?'

'Pathology samples.' She enjoyed the flicker of surprise in his eyes. 'From doctors' surgeries to the laboratories where they are tested. As I said before . . . Noah . . . I have friends in high places. I can get some of the business if I have a refrigerated truck,' she added triumphantly. 'Even if you can only give me a panel van, I'll get it refrigerated.'

He regarded her with a look of bemusement. 'I'll lend you one for a week. See how it goes.'

'A month,' she insisted. 'We'd need at least a month to get properly operational.'

A smile twitched at his lips. 'Very well. A month. As long as you agree that I can check the figures on the operation each week.'

'Fine!' She made an expansive gesture to show that his doubts didn't worry her at all.

'Fine!' he echoed, his quick grin beaming its unsettling wickedness. 'Happy now . . . Toni?'

'I can cross one more unemployed person off my list. Twenty still to go,' she said, reminding him once more of the depth of his perfidy before adding in a conciliatory tone, 'But I don't hate you nearly as much as I did.'

He laughed, his eyes simmering with something more than amusement as he removed his hands from his pockets, pushed himself away from the door, and strolled back towards her. Toni felt her nerves tensing with each step he took. She knew instinctively that his laugh boded no good for her, yet he had given in to her far more than she had expected. Surely that meant the victory was hers? The sense that he had somehow outmanoeuvred her seemed totally illogical.

'Now, my dear Miss Braden, I hope you'll agree that I've been of some service to you. So perhaps you'll feel it fair to do some little service for me,' he said silkily. His hands spread out in a gesture of inoffensive appeal as he came to a halt on the other side of her desk. 'Just as you said, it's a matter of learning. And I'm sure there's a lot I can learn from you. After all, you've had an experience I haven't had.'

'What's that?' Toni asked suspiciously.

'You've been married.'

'So?'

He had something up his sleeve. No matter how innocent he tried to look, there was definitely an evil glint in his eyes. His whole manner was fishy. Every alarm system Toni had was blinking red alert.

His reply was full of limpid simplicity. 'I want to know what mistakes to avoid when I get married. As I certainly intend to do in the not so distant future.'

He had set his mind on Jocelyn, then, Toni thought. Which was undoubtedly why he had conceded so much just now. But somehow the sense of power she had enjoyed fell rather flat as she considered the prospect of his marriage to her stepsister. Maybe he *would* get his own way. Maybe Dr Richard Gilbert didn't have what it took to wean Jocelyn away from a man as attractive as Noah Seton. Superficially attractive, she hastily amended. That cold computer mind was undoubtedly working at high-capacity level, waiting to dissect and correlate whatever she said.

He was coming closer to her. Right around the desk. He kept talking as if to divert her attention from the lessening of physical distance between them. 'I recall your saying that the idea of marriage is fine. It's what happens afterwards that's the problem. Would you be so kind as to elaborate on that statement? When the ceremony is over, what is it, in your opinion, that's wrong with marriage?'

He stopped so close to her that Toni had to tilt her head back to hold his gaze. To back away or look away would show weakness. Yet her whole nervous system shrieked imminent danger. She talked fast.

'Men see marriage as an end, not as a beginning. It's a stage in their lives——'

'You obviously chose the wrong partner,' he interpolated.

'And you wish to avoid that mistake?' she retorted derisively.

He shrugged. 'I'm trying. It's a gamble. Whichever way you look at it, there is an element of gambling involved.'

Why had his gaze flicked to her mouth just then? Why did she feel his words conveyed more than their surface meaning? Toni's pulse began to pound in her temples. She found her own gaze dropping to his mouth as it formed more words.

'But at least I'm starting with the percentages loaded the way I want them,' he said, his voice dropping to a deeper, softer tone.

He had firmly sculptured lips. Toni couldn't imagine them being sensitive at all. They seemed to be moving nearer as she stared at them. He was even affecting her focus, she thought dizzily, and forced her gaze up again. 'What percentages?' she mocked, trying to fight off the effect his nearness was having on her.

His head *was* bent towards hers. 'I want you to kiss me,' he said, the direct demand almost snatching Toni's breath away.

'Whatever for?' she gulped, caught between disbelief and the commanding intensity of those dark, mesmerising eyes.

'Assessment purposes.'

Toni was shocked. 'But you're going to marry Jocelyn!'

'Perhaps not.'

'What on earth are you saying?'

'"There is a tide in the affairs of men, Which, taken at the flood..."'

'You're quoting poetry at me again. And Shakespeare won't work for you either....' Her voice rose to a panicky squeak. He had put an arm around her and slid his hand up her spine to the nape of her neck, which he was caressing with a knowingly sensual touch. Toni swallowed hard to drive her voice down to a more authoritative level. 'I think——'

'Relax, Miss Braden... Toni. This is not going to hurt. It's no worse than going to the dentist.' The fingers of his other hand were fluttering down her face, arousing tingling sensations in confusing little trails.

Jocelyn was right, Toni thought distractedly. Sensitive. 'Only one kiss,' she breathed. All knowledge was useful, she assured herself wildly. 'And it has to be chaste,' she added, belatedly remembering Jocelyn's interests in this man.

'Of course,' he agreed, his gaze once more concentrated on her mouth as his face hovered above hers.

'As for a prospective sister-in-law,' she whispered.

'Exactly.'

Purely for assessment purposes, Toni recited, soothing her pricking conscience as his mouth began a studied offensive on hers. Besides, there was no definite commitment between him and Jocelyn. And there was Dr Richard Gilbert hovering in the wings. And the kiss was really quite chaste, only a seductive little graduation of pressures which she could respond to without any heartburn. Very pleasant. Definitely sensitive.

Toni wasn't quite sure when his mouth started to move more hungrily over hers. Things just seemed to escalate after the caressing fingers moved their attention from the nape of her neck and worked their way up through the thick mass of curls to support her head. And he was terribly good at what he was doing, his tongue flicking tantalising little caresses over the inner tissues of her lips . . . intensely sensual . . . exciting . . . tempting . . . It was only natural to respond . . . to taste how it could be if they carried the assessment a little deeper than chasteness.

Somehow, without actually meaning to, Toni lost control of the depth of experimentation. The explosive sensation of his tongue in her mouth caused a stream of fiery sweetness to race through her veins. She ceased to think, only feeling, and her own response was as violently needful as his possessive invasion. Toni forgot where she was, what she was supposed to be doing, and who was arousing her to such wild heights of urgent passion. Any space between them was crushed out of existence as their bodies instinctively sought their own satisfaction, the softness of her flesh revelling in the ungiving hardness of his, both making small shifts, adjustments, pushing the addictive excitement of more and more intimate contact as far as the barrier of clothes allowed.

And it wasn't just one kiss, although where one ended and the next began was not easy to define. Rather it was one long, mad continuity of whetting an increasingly greedy appetite for generating more intense nuances of sensation. Any idea of self-censorship had whirled off into Never-Never land and become hopelessly lost among swimming senses and clamouring needs. Toni actually made a bereft cry of protest when Noah pushed himself away from her. Her eyes flew open, and it came as a somewhat sobering shock to recognise the man who was shaking his head as if trying to force himself out of a daze.

'Dear heaven!' she gasped.

'Hell!' he groaned.

And Toni burned with the embarrassed remembrance of just how aroused he had been. And probably still was. In fact, it was just as well his hands were gripping her shoulders so hard or she might have melted on to the floor herself. There seemed to be no solid substance left inside her at all, and whatever there was still quivered with electric sensitivity.

'Wow!' she breathed, incredulity spreading another sort of glaze through her mind.

His eyes glittered into sharp focus, but his voice was still decidedly ragged as he attempted to mitigate what had happened between them. 'I didn't mean to do that, Toni. Not all of it, anyway.'

'I didn't exactly plan it myself,' she said in acknowledgement.

'Right!' He nodded jerkily. 'Just . . . one of those experiences. I'm glad I had it. I dare say . . . it happens all the time . . . with you.'

'Are you kidding?' The green eyes clearly expressed the fact that this had been a unique phenomenon for which she had no answer at all.

'Believe me, this is no kidding matter!' he said with a touch of grimness. 'Talk about the plans of mice and men——'

'Are you a quotation machine?' Toni demanded, beginning to recover her wits somewhat. 'First Wordsworth, then Shakespeare, now Steinbeck's novel! And that...that was supposed to be one chaste kiss for assessment purposes.'

'Yes. Well...' his quirky little smile held no apology at all '...I got a bit carried away with it.'

'A bit?'

'A lot,' he amended. 'But no harm done...is there?'

'I...guess not,' she agreed, although in some considerable confusion of mind about it.

'Fine!' He touched her cheek in brief salute. 'Best of luck with the re-employment programme. I'll get the refrigerated truck to you tomorrow.'

He had left her standing, and was already opening the office door before Toni could fully grasp the fact that he was actually walking out on her. 'Wait!' she called, unable to accept this...wholesale desertion after...

'Yes?' He looked back enquiringly at her, his face reset in perfectly controlled lines.

A sense of outrage put some stiffening into Toni's spine. Her hands leapt to her hips, adding their strength and support to her stance. 'The least you can do is tell me your assessment. Since I lent myself so generously to your purpose,' she said with acid bite.

'That seems fair,' he agreed, then frowned in simulated consideration. Pure wickedness glittered in his eyes when he lifted his head to deliver his judgement. 'I'd have to say ninety-two per cent,' he drawled.

'Ninety-two?' To Toni's mind that was an out-and-out insult. It should have been a hundred plus at least!

He grinned. 'Very high. I'll see you next week, Toni. To check the figures on the courier service.'

He was out of the office with the door shut behind him before she could think of a cutting enough remark to hurl back at him. She didn't even have any satisfactory object to throw after him. Toni was left burning with a multitude of frustrations, some of which she didn't want to dwell on too closely in case she started to feel humiliated. Her self-esteem didn't need that kind of negative blow.

Her mind issued forth a whole stream of positive resolutions. She would get back at Noah Seton. She would make him crawl for her favours. She would crack his control so far that he would be begging for mercy.

And then she remembered Jocelyn, and all the delicious fantasies collapsed like punctured balloons. For once in her life, Toni didn't know what to do.

CHAPTER FIVE

'NO HARM done...' Noah Seton's words slipped into Toni's mind, and with typical vigour and determination she adopted them as her own and went to work on them. She had placed seven people. That was an achievement to be proud of. How could a kiss be even compared to it? She certainly had no intention whatsoever of encroaching on Jocelyn's territory. It was simply a matter of perspective. Accidents happened. She had no control over events like that. And of course she would ensure that similar circumstances did not arise in the future.

Toni reached for the telephone and plunged herself into the happy task of spreading good news. She left six families feeling a lot more cheerful, and shot a bright ray of optimism into the seventh with the plan for the courier business. By the time she locked up the office and headed for home, she had recovered the natural spring in her step. Indeed, there was so much of her inner vitality shining through that the attendant at the parking station where she had left her car was delighted to help her find the vehicle again.

A sense of direction, she reflected, was not one of her strong points. Not that it mattered, because people were always so kind in showing her where to go. Quite often men accompanied her all the way, just to make sure she reached her destination safely. But then most men had more humanity than Noah Seton!

Ninety-two per cent! That really rankled! Particularly when... but she wasn't going to think about that. It was just... one of those things... an experience... and she was glad she'd had it . . . but it was totally unimportant. Sexual attraction could play those tricks on you—here today, gone tomorrow—no basis at all for a deep and lasting relationship. And Noah Seton had well and truly proved he was nothing but a cold, calculating computer . . . coming up with a nasty ninety-two per cent! What more did he want, for heaven's sake? But she wasn't going to think about that!

Her car negotiated the traffic over the Sydney Harbour Bridge and found its own way to her home in Mosman. Toni looked up at Ray's beautiful old mansion with a sense of surprise. She had hardly noticed any of the trip across the city.

This home had been in Ray's family for three generations and it was certainly impressive. It was set in huge grounds and had views of Sydney Harbour from practically every window. Worth millions, her ex-husband had told her, but Toni hadn't seen the gleam of avarice in his eyes at that early point in their relationship. She wondered if Dr Richard Gilbert had found it daunting to his prospects with Jocelyn. The recollection of his words—'I shouldn't have come here'—niggled at her mind. Would he let Jocelyn's wealthy background stop him from pursuing his interest in her?

Surely doctors earned a comfortable income? Toni reasoned. Every doctor she knew appeared to be quite wealthy. Admittedly, Richard Gilbert was still rather young, but with such an assured career ahead of him he could hardly be called destitute. If Jocelyn's background was a stumbling-block, then the good doctor was a wimp, Toni concluded. Unfortunately the conclusion didn't give her much joy.

What joy she had was substantially diminished at the dinner-table. 'Where's Jocelyn?' she asked—a trifle concerned—when only Ray joined her for the meal.

'She called earlier to say she would be out,' Ray answered, his expression of benevolence given an extra shine as he added, 'A date with Noah, I expect.'

Toni's appetite took an abrupt downturn. In fact, her stomach seemed to curdle. That Noah Seton should go from her... and... Toni felt decidedly sick.

'How did your day go, my dear?' Ray asked, his eyes alight with interest.

Apparently he couldn't see that she was green around the gills. Toni rallied herself to give a triumphant account of her business acumen so far.

Ray's face beamed with pleasure. 'How good of Noah to be so obliging!'

Which instantly spoiled all Toni's pleasure.

'It shows a side to him which I wasn't sure existed,' Ray continued musingly. 'An extremely good businessman, of course. Outstanding. But I'm glad to see he makes allowances for personal interest. It assures me that he will look after Jocelyn's happiness should they get married.'

It was obvious that Ray didn't have a clue to Noah Seton's true nature, Toni thought. Consideration for Ray's feelings prevented her from disillusioning him. She didn't feel right about it. She didn't feel right about anything.

'Antonia...'

She looked up to find his eyes boring a direct appeal at her.

'...Noah has asked that all three of us join him at his country home for the weekend after next. You might recall it's near Bowral. I'm inclined to think he has planned that occasion for... well, I wouldn't be surprised if an announcement was made during the course of the weekend. I think you should be there, Antonia.'

'No!' The sharp negative was out before she could catch it back, but the thought of Noah Seton going ahead with a marriage to Jocelyn made her feel even sicker. 'I can't, Ray. I've made other plans,' she added quickly.

He frowned, obviously disappointed.

'If he's proposing to Jocelyn, he won't miss me,' she said with bitter logic.

Ray sighed. 'It's a matter of family, Antonia. And since Noah has gone out of his way to help you in your enterprise...please give it some more thought, my dear.'

She couldn't explain how churned up she felt about it. If Noah Seton hadn't kissed her... And why had he done that if he intended to marry Jocelyn? It made no sense.

Fortunately, Ray did not press her any further. After a few minutes, when she hadn't said anything, he changed the subject. 'And how is the money coming in, my dear?' he asked, a slight touch of benevolence in his question.

'I didn't make any today. I was only starting on the spadework,' she explained. 'And I couldn't charge Noah Seton for those six people, because I didn't do any work to place them. But don't worry, Ray. It's coming. Everything is falling into place.'

She had put in some very pointed spadework, Toni thought to herself with grim satisfaction, and Noah Seton would certainly be paying for it before too long. She would show him just how calculating she could be, when she put her mind to it. And he would learn a salutary lesson about running a transport business. Computers had their place, but so did people!

She forced herself to make a fair stab at the meal, so as not to upset Mrs Frobisher or draw any more uncomfortable questions from Ray, then quickly excused herself from the table.

With each step she took up the stairs to her room, Toni resolved not to think about Noah Seton...with Jocelyn. A proper perspective had to be maintained, she recited to herself. She would think about Lillian Devereux's plan to help the deaf children. Some brilliant scheme was needed to raise lots of money. She wondered if they could rob Noah Seton and get away with it. Take him over. Leave *him* destitute. Unfortunately she couldn't see him turning into a wimp. With his calculating mind he would probably make another fortune in no time flat!

Toni paced the floor in her bedroom, trying to concentrate her mind on ideas for Lillian's charity. She was concentrating so hard that she just about wore out the carpet, but inspiration was sadly lacking. She wondered if Ray and Lillian might made a good pair—solve each other's problems—then promptly ruled it out. When Henry Devereux had died, Lillian had sworn she would never have a *man* in her house again. Not under any pretext. Toni wondered why people were so inflexible.

The hours ticked on by. Jocelyn still wasn't home. Not that that was any of Toni's business. Jocelyn had every right to stay out as late as she liked.

Since her mind was not proving fertile on ideas, and she couldn't figure out if Ray and Lillian might get along together, Toni decided she had better go to bed and sleep on the problem. Tomorrow was another day. Tomorrow she would really get herself moving on everything—get the paint, find more jobs, choose some carpet. By the time Noah Seton came back next week she would have her office in great shape!

Bed, however, did not turn out to be a good idea. Bed had an inevitable association with sex. And not even her ex-husband—at his very best—had ever stirred the kind of wild arousal Toni had experienced this afternoon. It was very unsettling. She couldn't relax, no matter how hard she tried. Her sheets were in a frustrating tangle when she heard Jocelyn come home. The luminous numerals on the bedside clock pulsed out at Toni...12.55! If Noah Seton was still playing the gentleman with Jocelyn, that was a hell of a long day for him!

Toni hurled away the twisted sheets, leapt out of bed and stormed along to Jocelyn's bedroom, driven by an overwhelming need to know the worst. Then she could come to terms with it, she reasoned wildly.

Jocelyn hadn't closed her door. Toni came to an abrupt halt as she caught sight of her stepsister standing dreamily in front of the dresing-table mirror, one finger lightly tracing over her lips as if trying to recapture sensations that other lips had left there. Toni felt as if an iron fist had closed around her heart. It started to squeeze painfully when Jocelyn's hand dropped to her breast and held it as if it was unbearably tender.

'Not so cold tonight?'

Something terribly black had rolled over Toni's mind. She vaguely identified it as blind fury. Jealousy was something she had never experienced before. But pounding through the blackness was the thought that Noah Seton had warmed up his passions on her and then transferred them to Jocelyn...

Her stepsister jerked around, her hand quickly fluttering down, her face flushing in guilty-looking embarrassment. 'Oh, Toni...I...no, it's not cold.'

'I meant Noah Seton,' Toni bit out, unable to stop herself.

'Noah?' Jocelyn's blush deepened. 'I wasn't with Noah tonight, Toni. I went out with a friend from the hospital.'

The black wave receded into an odd blankness. 'You haven't been with him?'

'Who?' Jocelyn looked evasive.

'Noah Seton!' Toni almost yelled at her.

Jocelyn shook her head in puzzlement at her step-sister's strange behaviour. 'I haven't seen Noah since the party,' she said, unable to put it more plainly.

Toni tried to straighten out her whirling mind, but the situation just didn't add up straight. 'Why not?' she demanded.

Jocelyn frowned at her. 'Why not what? Is something wrong, Toni? You're up late. Can't you sleep?'

Nothing made sense. Why had Jocelyn been touching herself like that if...? A shaft of hope pierced Toni's turbulent soul. 'Was it Richard?'

'What do you mean?' Jocelyn again looked evasive.

'Richard...the doctor...your friend from the hospital,' Toni cried impatiently.

'Oh!' Jocelyn's face was a picture of guilty pleasure. 'Yes...as a matter of fact it was. He asked me out and...well, we've been friends for a long time. I couldn't see any harm in it,' Jocelyn mumbled self-consciously.

'No. No harm at all,' Toni agreed on a huge wave of relief. 'That's fine...really fine, Jocelyn. Keep it up,' she added somewhat incoherently. 'Goodnight.'

Back in her own room, Toni had no trouble at all in getting to sleep. She felt like a sponge that had been squeezed dry. She lay limply on the bed and surrendered herself to oblivion.

When she woke the next morning, refreshed in mind and body, Toni started to zing again. She did not let any thought of Noah Seton trouble her in the least. After all, Richard Gilbert couldn't possibly be a wimp if he had put that wondering glow on Jocelyn's face. And the refrigerated truck turned up, demonstrating that Noah Seton was as good as his word. Although why that pleased her she wasn't quite sure.

She made copious notes on all her clients' skills and ambitions, and assured them that their job prospects were excellent. The only blot on her schedule was Mr Templeton's failure to keep his appointment. He didn't answer his telephone either. Concerned that the poor old dear might have fallen ill, Toni resolved to visit his home as soon as she finished work for the day.

Having called Mrs Frobisher to ask her not to wait dinner on her, she closed up the office at five o'clock, and set off for the address Mr Templeton had given her. It turned out to be a neatly kept terraced house, near a pleasant little park at Croydon. To her surprise and relief, Mr Templeton answered her knock almost straight away.

He was dressed in his business suit, as if he had just returned home from work. His face wore the dreamy expression of living in another world. Mr Templeton always gave the impression that anything that happened to him or anyone else was always a total surprise.

'Miss Braden...' he greeted her in some embarrassment. 'I'm sorry you've put yourself out. There wasn't any point in my coming in. I tried to ring you, but your telephone always seemed to be engaged. I'm sorry——'

'My fault, Mr Templeton,' she cut in, cheerfully accepting the blame. 'I simply dropped by in case you'd taken ill. Or broken a leg.'

'How kind! Please...you must come in now you're here. I must make it up to you for all your trouble. Perhaps you would dine with me, if you don't have to hurry away?' he added hopefully.

'If it wouldn't be too much trouble, I'll take you up on that, Mr Templeton,' Toni agreed, aware of how lonely he must have been since his invalid wife had died a year ago. And now with his job lost and the companionship of old workmates gone also, he had to be lonelier than ever. Apart from that, she could now do the interview he had missed out on this morning.

'I hope you don't mind sitting in the kitchen while I cook,' he fussed self-consciously as they moved down the dark narrow hallway.

Toni laughed. 'As long as you don't expect me to cook, Mr Templeton, that suits me fine. I'm totally useless at it.'

'Would you like me to teach you?' he offered eagerly.

'It's a conscious decision on my part, Mr Templeton. I don't want to learn.' Toni grinned to dispel any offence in her statement.

He chuckled. 'I enjoy it anyway. I used to prepare all the meals for my wife, you know. She wasn't well enough to cope with cooking.'

He really was a dear, Toni thought, as he bustled around the kitchen, chopping up herbs and shallots, beating eggs, and being generally very domestic. She hoped his wife had appreciated such a gem of a husband...steady, dependable, caring. He was meticulous in cleaning everything and putting it away after he had used it—exactly the same tidy mannerisms that had made him so dependable at the transport company.

He wasn't bad-looking for fifty-five years of age: tall, a bit stooped about the shoulders from all the book-keeping he had done, a trifle on the thin side, but he had a fine thatch of iron-grey hair, large, soulful grey eyes, and his face carried that other-world look of being completely divorced from all the woes and sorrows of this life. Saintly, thought Toni, described him very well.

She doubted that he had ever had the kind of magnetic presence that Noah Seton achieved without any exertion at all, but Mr Templeton would surely have attracted women all his life. He had such beautiful old-world manners. It was really quite a delight to share a meal with him.

He finished setting the table for them, took off his apron, hung it on a peg behind the door, then faced Toni with a serious confidential air. 'There truly was no point to my coming in this morning, you know, Miss Braden.'

'You've found a job?' Toni asked, noting his business suit once more.

'No, my dear. But I've looked life in the face. I am unemployable.'

'That's not true!' Toni denied vehemently.

He gestured his hopelessness. 'What can I do?'

'That's what I wanted to talk to you about. What are your interests, your hobbies?'

He grimaced. 'I haven't any really. I potter around the garden. I like growing things. But the reality is that, in this age of computers, I'm a displaced person.'

He turned aside, opened the oven, removed a casserole dish and proceeded to serve the tuna soufflé he had made on to their plates. 'Don't look so distressed, my dear,' he advised Toni as she looked glumly at the food. 'We all have to face up to reality one day.'

Toni had just remembered one reality. She was not particularly partial to tuna. At the present moment, listening to Mr Templeton, she wasn't particularly hungry. But she would die rather than offend him. With determined good will, she started in on the meal the moment he was seated. To her startled pleasure the tuna soufflé was unbelievably good.

'The best I've ever tasted!' she declared with absolute sincerity. 'Quite superb! In a category with Mrs Frobisher's masterpieces!'

Mr Templeton glowed with pleasure. 'My wife used to say that no one had a lighter touch with a soufflé. I must admit I do pride myself on them. It's a pity I can't get myself a job as a chef. But I'm too old now. Couldn't stand it physically. Rushing meals in restaurants and late nights. Should have done it when I was young.'

His face fell into gloom as he considered his future. 'No one will want a fifty-five-year-old book-keeper, Miss Braden. Computers finished me. I'm outdated. Lived past my usefulness. I don't want you to trouble yourself on my account. It will be a good thing to give up this house. Too many memories of my wife...and old times. I'll rent myself a room somewhere...go on the pension...you mustn't worry about me. You have your own life to live. And I don't want to be a trouble to anyone any more.'

Toni barely heard his last words. Her mind was bursting from one idea to the next with all the fabulous explosiveness of a fireworks display. And it was the perfect answer to everything Lillian Devereux wanted! However, there was one stumbling-block. First she had to persuade Lillian to accept a man into her household, and that was going to take a good deal of tactical manoeuvring. It needed careful thought and even more careful handling! Toni did not doubt for a moment that she would find a way. It was only a matter of time.

'Mr Templeton...' Her green eyes sparkled with triumph, forbidding him anything but a positive response. 'I've got exactly the right place for you. There are one or two problems that have yet to be sorted out. But I'll get that done. Just give me a week and it will be all systems go.'

His face puckered in concern. 'My dear, you mustn't let your dreams carry you away.'

Toni laughed and reached across the table to squeeze his hand. 'I assure you I'm not being fanciful, Mr Templeton. This is the kind of job that'll give you a new lease of life. You'll be able to cook your lovely meals for one of the kindest women in the world...and do a few other little services that you have the perfect image for. When I get this all arranged, promise me you'll give it a go.'

He looked stunned.

'Let me set up an interview. If it's not everything I promise, you can always say no,' Toni pressed eagerly. 'But you have to promise to give it a chance.'

'Well...I don't suppose an interview could do any harm,' he acknowledged, but the scepticism in his manner implied that he saw no hope anywhere.

'No harm at all,' Toni reinforced the idea. She leapt out of her chair, danced around the table and planted an exuberant kiss on Mr Templeton's astonished face. 'Now promise me you won't back out!' she insisted. 'This is very important to me.'

'Important to you, my dear Miss Braden?'

She looked him in the eye with earnest conviction. 'I can't explain until I've got everything arranged, but cross my heart, Mr Templeton, this is one of the most important things I've ever done. And I desperately need your co-operation!'

'Well, then...if that's the case... Yes, I promise,' he agreed, his face quite suffused with pleasure.

She gave him a hug of approval. 'Thank you for the lovely meal. I must be off. I'll ring you about the interview when I get it all lined up.'

'Don't work overtime for me, Miss Braden,' he called after her as she whirled down the hallway.

'Oh, I will. I will,' she chanted in her elation, leaving Mr Templeton in a state of utter bemusement.

Toni would have loved to rush straight off to Lillian Devereux, but she determinedly restrained the impulse. She promised herself she would take at least three days to work out the best plan of approach and polish it to perfection. She couldn't allow one loophole in it or Lillian might not agree. Toni simply couldn't countenance that happening.

She had so much to do and so much to think about over the next few days that she didn't have time to monitor what was going on between Jocelyn and Richard and Noah Seton, if indeed anything was going on at all. In any case, she decided that Noah Seton didn't deserve to be thought of, and whenever he slid into her mind she kicked him out again.

Unfortunately, when he burst into her office on Friday afternoon, without so much as a knock or a by-your-leave, Toni was not in a position to kick him out, or even reprimand him for his discourtesy. She was stretched out on the floor, painting the terracotta pot which held the rhododendron the same lovely moss-green she had painted the window-frame and the skirting-board.

She had been happily rehearsing what she was going to say to Lillian Devereux this evening, and now her whole train of thought was ruined. She glared at Noah Seton in fierce resentment. He not only had no right to come into her office like that, he had no right to be here at all.

'We agreed on a week, Mr Seton,' she snapped. 'This is Friday, not Monday!'

The stinging truth of her words arrested him, which gave Toni some satisfaction. It still chagrined her that he had caught her in such an undignified position, and wearing her old boiler-suit, an outdated raggy cheese-cloth one-piece that covered her from neck to foot and had long fitted sleeves—ideal for painting, but abysmal for her businesswoman image. She had tied a bright multi-coloured scarf around her waist—not even a belt—and those magnetic dark eyes of his were moving over her, undoubtedly picking up every paint-spot splattered on the lipstick-pink cheesecloth.

He, of course, looked sickeningly suave and elegant in a light grey suit that had a sheen of silk about it. It was decidedly unfair. Toni wished she could have daubed him over with her paintbrush just to even things up. That, however, would not compensate for the fact that she was barefoot and he was outfitted in hand-crafted soft Italian leather shoes.

All in all, Toni found it very difficult to see how she was going to achieve any dignity, let alone match up to the image being projected by Noah Seton. Her shoes were on the desk with the rest of her proper clothes, except for her tights, which were tied around the rhododendron to keep the leaves out of the wet paint on the pot. The only course of action open to her was to carry off the situation with supreme nonchalance. Having resolved that in her mind, Toni put down her paintbrush and rose to her feet with her best attempt at careless grace.

The constructed look of lofty disdain on her face was absolutely wasted on Noah Seton. His gaze was fastened with intense scrutiny on some point between her breasts. Toni recollected that she hadn't done all the buttons up. Damn! She should have worn a bra after all, she thought in exasperation. Things were going from bad to worse! To her considerable discomfort she felt her nipples hardening. Double damn the man!

She did up the offending buttons with a disdainful movement of her hand. Noah Seton's eyes stil did not appear to be properly focused. Toni was pricklingly aware that her breasts were now jutting pointedly against the flimsy cheesecloth. Why didn't the wretched man speak...tell her what he had come about?

Her mind suddenly latched on to the possibility that the seeds she had spread around the transport industry might have borne fruit much earlier than she had expected. If so, dignity was well lost for the victory she confidently anticipated.

'I was not expecting you today, Mr Seton,' she said smoothly, impatient to know if she was right. 'What can I do for you?'

His chin lifted slightly as his eyes finally found a direct line to hers. His face tightened. His jaw clenched so hard that she saw muscles in his cheeks contract.

'I'm sure you know why, Miss Braden,' he rasped. 'You're the prime mover in what has happened. I can see your hand in it all the way back to day one. I have no doubt whatsoever that you're fully aware of what you've done and the inevitable repercussions. I'm also certain that, when you determined to be a thorn in my side, you calculated the depth of every wound, every scratch.'

A triumphant smile spread across her face, illuminating it with a vibrancy that would have stopped traffic anywhere. 'Has someone thrown a spanner in the works, Mr Seton?' she asked, unable to resist taking his arrogance down a peg or two. 'I take it you've discovered that it's not nearly as easy to run the business as you thought. And you've come to realise that some people are *necessary* to running the enterprise successfully.'

He made no reply.

Toni got carried away with elation at her success. 'If you've come to re-employ a few more people, Mr Seton, then thank you for thinking of those you fired. Just let me get my notebook so I can tick off the names and then we can get straight down to business. And what it's going to cost you.'

Still no reply. Noah Seton looked as if he had turned into stone. Whatever was on his mind was completely walled off from her. Toni had a moment's disquiet about his total lack of reaction, but the die was cast now. She walked over to the desk and got out her notebook, not doubting for a second that victory was hers.

CHAPTER SIX

NOAH SETON was in two minds. It was not a state he enjoyed. He knew what he had come to do...what he ought to do...what anyone in his right mind would do. Antonia Braden needed to be taught a stringent lesson. He could tie her up in legal knots. He could trim her sails so hard that she would never skim over water again. He could squash that light in her eyes in ten seconds flat. To even hesitate about doing it proved he was not in his right mind.

He had been fair. He had been more than fair, taking back six of the employees and giving her the use of the refrigerated truck! Although, if he was completely honest with himself, he had agreed to the truck in order to pave the way for...that explosive kiss! He had meant to assert his control over the temptation she embodied and, instead of that, the memory of the volcanic excitement she had evoked had disrupted his concentration all week.

Why did she affect him like that? It was unreasonable! There ought to be a law against women like her. Just now he had gone so far as to gawk at her breasts like a schoolboy. And he had to stop admiring the sheer audacity of her mind. She was devious, tricky and conniving...yet she had a flair for business that he wished some of his general managers had. But he could hardly excuse what she had done this week on the count of this stupid fascination she cast over him.

He had no problem at all making up his mind about Jocelyn. That was completely clear-cut now. And he would take the proper steps over the appropriate period of time. But this little packet of dynamite... what was he going to do about her? The thoughts that kept going through his mind... well, that was impossible!

When Toni looked up from her noteook, Noah Seton's face still looked as if it were carved from granite, but his expression had changed. The sternness and disapproval were blistering indictments of what she had done, but, more than that, there was something implacable in those dark eyes that made her want to crawl into a hole and hide.

For the first time she wondered if she had gone too far. Noah Seton had been good to her... gone out of his way to appease and help her. Even if it had only been to tidy up his relationship with Jocelyn, he had still been generous. And she didn't really want to make an enemy of him. Not unnecessarily. Not totally. In actual fact, she had made those damaging calls before he had come with his peace-offerings on Monday. Although, if she was honest with herself, she had been intent on making them anyway. Because he was wrong! Nevertheless, she didn't feel too right with him looking at her like that.

It was a sobering thought. Her sense of triumph dwindled into something rather miserable. In an attempt to lighten the atmosphere and inject a brighter note into proceedings, she drew his attention to the other things she had done. 'What do you think of my office now?' she asked, waving towards the bright paintwork and the new carpet.

He took his time looking around before returning his gaze to her. 'Anything would have been an improvement,' he said grimly.

'You don't like it?'

His eyes mocked her persistence. 'It's starting to look . . . homey.'

The sardonic tone was little better than his grimness. There was no avoiding the real issue, and Toni acknowledged she might as well get on with it. 'You're obviously aware . . .' she said judiciously ' . . . that I've been in contact with certain people and you're going to lose a lot of business if you don't re-employ certain people.'

'That's why I'm here. I've been informed by the extra men I wish to employ that you will negotiate their re-employment. So how much do you want this time, Toni?'

She flinched at the sting in those last words. It was all his own fault, Toni swiftly argued to herself. He had arrogantly overlooked the strength of loyalties, and dismissed the comfortable bond of working relationships that had been forged from years of dealing with good will. New management couldn't possibly be as effective as old employees who were tuned into the special needs of customers. Noah Seton deserved to pay for that mistake.

Having bolstered her resolve, Toni began her bargaining spiel. 'You have to consider personal hardship, distress, wounded feelings, insult to ego——'

'Spare me the details,' he cut in, his eyes glittering with derision.

'Three months' wages for each of them,' she demanded defiantly.

'I'm surprised you're letting me off so lightly,' he drawled.

Her chin came up. 'Plus the same for myself as commission.'

His mouth tightened.

Perhaps she had gone too far, Toni thought ruefully. But he had goaded her into it. 'Ray said I had to make a profit,' she defended.

'A cheque will be in the mail on Monday,' he said, and the chill in his voice sent a shiver down Toni's spine.

Something was wrong. Badly wrong. He was giving in to her demands far too easily. He should have been talking, trying to change her mind, get her to take less. Something was wrong.

Toni's intuition shrieked that there were going to be repercussions from this meeting...things she hadn't foreseen. She didn't believe that Noah Seton wouldn't fight for every inch of what he considered his territory. So either he was acting completely out of character or... had she done some terrible damage?

'Noah...'

One of his eyebrows kicked up in sardonic enquiry. Toni flushed as she realised she had used his first name, but the matter was too urgent to be bothered about something as trivial as that.

'...this doesn't change anything between you and Jocelyn, does it?' As much as she hoped he would not be Jocelyn's choice in the end, she had no right to interfere with their relationship.

'Not a thing,' he replied without a moment's hesitation.

Toni smothered the disquiet she felt at this declaration that his interest in Jocelyn was unchanged. 'This is just between you and me,' she pleaded.

'Absolutely,' he agreed. 'And, while we're on the subject, I want those men back at work on Monday. I presume you know which four.'

She named them and he nodded. His mouth twisted into a mocking little smile. 'You can now tick them off your list.'

'Yes. Thank you,' she said in some confusion. Something was definitely going on here that she didn't understand, but she ticked off the names and closed her notebook.

'So how many are left now?' he asked, still with that quirky smile on his lps.

Toni wasn't sure what he meant by it, but she answered in a straightforward fashion. 'Thirteen. I placed two others this week, and I expect to fix Mr Templeton up tonight.'

'You must be feeling pleased with yourself,' he said, strolling towards her.

Toni stood her ground. It wasn't a menacing approach. The expression on his face was self-mocking. Certainly not threatening. Yet a quivery sensation filtered through Toni's body as he came closer... and closer. She didn't think he meant to kiss her again, and of course she didn't want him to, but his nearness evoked memories that clouded her mind, making the passage of any thought a difficult business.

'I won't trouble you any more about them,' she said thickly.

He half dropped his lids, hooding the gathering glitter in his eyes. 'I know you won't. The doors are now closed on that account.' His gaze simmered down to her mouth.

Her lips started to tremble. She compressed them and swallowed hard, fighting the gathering constriction in her throat. 'The courier service... with the

refrigerated truck...it's looking good,' she choked
out.

'I'm glad to hear it,' he murmured. He pulled his
gaze back up to hers. 'I'll come around next Tuesday
to check on how it's going.'

'Fine,' she whispered.

He lifted his hand and softly stroked a finger down
her nose. 'You've got a spot of paint there. Better
clean it off before going out to fix up Mr Templeton.
Otherwise, he will think you somewhat less than
professional.'

The finger dropped to the deep indentation of her
upper lip, lingered there a moment, then was removed. Without another word he turned away and
strode towards the door, leaving Toni in a state of
absolute turmoil. He made his exit without a
backward glance, going out as swiftly as he had come
in, and Toni just stood there like a stunned mullet
and watched him go.

There was no point in denying the awful truth now.
She had wanted him to kiss her. She had wanted to
feel that wild passion again. And she hated him for
leaving her strung out on a limb with all her nerve-
ends screeching in frustration. She hated herself for
wanting what she shouldn't want. He was Jocelyn's
man and Noah Seton was not about to change that.
He had told her so straight out.

The kiss they had shared meant nothing to him.
Just a brief aberration that he had obviously dismissed. Toni suddenly realised why he had come close
to her and touched her like that. He had remembered
her vulnerability to him and used it deliberately to
taunt her...putting her down in the only way he
could...his nasty little revenge for the victory she had
scored off him.

The more she thought about it, the more Toni fumed. Her only consolation was that she had made him pay as much as he had, even to the outrageous commission she had demanded. Although she still didn't understand why he had given in to her claims without so much as a protest, let alone an argument. There was something fishy about it, as if he had a hidden joker up his sleeve, waiting to be dealt at a later date. No matter how hard Toni tried to recapture a feeling of triumph, it completely eluded her. Not even the telephone calls to the four men could lift her spirits, although they were most appreciative of what she had done for them.

She felt too disgruntled to enjoy painting any more. Noah Seton had ruined that too. But she finished the pot, determined not to let *him* disrupt her plans. Then she cleaned everything up, including the minuscule paint-spot on her nose, and changed back into the clothes she had chosen for her visit to Lillian.

She cast a look of satisfaction around her office before locking up, wrinkling her nose in disgust at Noah Seton's descripton of 'homey'. The improvements she had made were brilliant. Anyone who came to her for help would certainly be lifted out of any depression simply by soaking in the bright ambience of her office. Noah Seton's problem was that he couldn't see further than his own interests.

He wouldn't be bothered putting *his* mind to solving the problem of raising money for the deaf children. He would probably have no idea of how to go about it anyway. People like him had little or no originality at all. Perhaps a little. But on the whole they lived their lives in controlled strait-jackets, their minds fixed in narrow one-way lanes.

Toni embellished these thoughts as she drove through the city towards the eastern suburbs. By the time she arrived at Lillian Devereux's home at Pott's Point, she had managed to relegate Noah Seton to a distant back-burner that would eventually be quenched.

Lillian herself answered the doorbell. The eagerness in her eyes told Toni better than words that much was expected of this visit, even though Toni had said very little on the telephone. She had only done a selective bit of hinting to whet Lillian's interest.

'I knew you would think of something!' Lillian gushed excitedly as she ushered Toni into the informal lounge-room—so called, but not anything like it in reality. Every feature—furnishings, ornaments, floral arrangements—was precise, fussy, over-endowed. It bespoke an exactitude of mind, an over-femininity, an obsession about everything being just so. In a curious kind of way, it reminded Toni of Mr Templeton's kitchen.

Lillian urged her into a chintzy armchair then moved quickly to a small lace-covered table where she had placed a crystal decanter of sherry and exquisitely dainty little glasses. 'You'll have a sherry with me, won't you, Toni?' she invited pressingly. 'I always have one or two at this hour.'

'Thank you, I will,' Toni agreed quickly. Lillian would probably need a shot of alcohol once she heard the proposition Toni was going to give her. Sherry was definitely a good idea.

As Toni accepted her glass and waited for Lillian to settle down, she adjusted her face to its most solemn. What she had come about was more than serious. She was going to tread on sacrosanct ground.

Lillian looked at her expectantly. 'So what is it?' she asked, twinkling with anticipation.

'Mrs Devereux...Lillian...we need to begin at the beginning,' Toni said earnestly. 'We are agreed—we have to be—that men on the whole are vile creatures. Husbands are the worst. Essentially they are pigs!'

Lillian's initial look of surprise faded into a shudder of distaste. 'Henry...' was all she said, but it was enough to indicate that the memory of Henry did not sit pleasantly on her shoulders.

'I also, as you know, have had the most distasteful of life's experiences,' Toni said cheerfully, feeling she was in total empathy with the woman sitting opposite her. 'One that we women can happily turn our backs on.'

Lillian nodded sympathetically.

This was going even better than Toni had expected. She hesitated for dramatic effect. 'I've come up with an idea that will raise the money for the bionic ear operations. However, it will require you to make an enormous sacrifice, Lillian. It's the only way it can be done. I'd make it myself—for the sake of the deaf children—but I'm afraid it can only be you. Or the scheme won't work.'

Lillian looked perplexed.

Toni took a deep breath and projected desperate appeal. 'I need you to take a man into your life and household.'

'Toni!' Shock and horror flitted across Lillian's face. 'I couldn't...it's too much...'

Toni instantly employed relief. '*Only* as a cook. Not as a husband.'

Bewilderment ensued. 'I...I don't understand...'

Toni hitched herself forward and spoke with intense conviction. 'It's simple, really. The other night

I thought that what we needed was an auction. But not like any other auction that we have ever done.'

Interest was rekindled. 'What do you have in mind?'

'Let's start with the negatives. The way things normally are.' Toni grimaced her boredom and disapproval with that. 'You know how it is. Most charity auctions put up...say, refrigerators at a thousand dollars. What happens? They bring a thousand, or nine hundred, or eleven hundred. There's no leverage. And leverage is what we've got to get.'

'How do you intend to get it?' Lillian pressed curiously.

Toni grinned. 'Between ourselves we'll call it "The Tycoons' Bloodbath"! For the outside world we'll name it "Fantasy of Fantasies". We're going to auction some of the most useless things in the world and watch some of the wealthiest men scrabble like little children to outdo one another. We're going to place their egos on the line...watch them fight it out...I suppose like mad bulls going at one another. You know what I mean. This is the plan...'

Lillian listened with awed delight as Toni outlined the strategy and what had to be done to achieve the end they wanted. 'My dear! You are a genius!' she cried, cock-a-hoop at the certainty that the money would come rolling in, just as Toni predicted.

'But we need Mr Templeton,' Toni reminded her gently.

'Yes...yes, I can see that...' Reluctance dragged at her voice.

'And what he wants is a job as a personal cook. If you take him on, Lillian, we've got the scheme sewn up. He'll do anything we ask him to. Eat out of our hands. Otherwise...' Toni sighed heavily and lifted her hands in a gesture of helplessness. 'Otherwise how can I guarantee it?'

A shudder ran through Lillian's body. She took a stiff swallow of sherry—finished the glass—then rose to something over her sturdy five feet in height . . . a picture of decision.

'For this cause, I'll do it!' she declared with absolute determination.

It was the ultimate sacrifice.

Toni stood up in respect. 'You're a wonderful woman, Lillian. I'll bring Mr Templeton over tomorrow so you can see that he's everything I said he was. You can give him the interview and agree to employ him. It's not a total loss. He does cook superbly well.'

'What has to be done, has to be done,' Lillian said in saintly resignation.

Toni began to think that Lillian and Mr Templeton might make a perfect match, but there was no point in overdoing things. She had achieved what she had set out to achieve. She took her leave of Lillian and drove away in high spirits. This was one triumph that Noah Seton could not spoil. She could hardly wait to get home so she could ring Mr Templeton and tell him the good news.

However, no sooner was she in the front door than she was accosted by Ray, coming out of the library with a face that was stripped of all benevolence. He looked almost grey with strain and worry.

'Antonia, please . . . a private word with you,' he demanded with uncharacteristic concern.

'What's wrong?' she cried, alarmed by his look of illness. 'Can I get a doctor?'

He didn't reply. He waved her into the library with tight-lipped grimness. Toni hurried forward, anxious to know what had caused such a change in him. This morning at breakfast he had been his normal self. He had eaten his marmalade with relish. Something dreadful must have happened.

'Jocelyn!' she cried, whirling on him in frightened enquiry as he followed her in and closed the door.

His eyes stabbed at her in pained reproach. 'Jocelyn, I am thankful to say, is not causing me any concern. But you, Antonia... how could you have been so... so irresponsible?'

'Me?' she squeaked, the wind knocked completely out of her sails.

'I know you were upset by the take-over,' he shot at her with more passion than she had ever heard from him. 'I know you were disappointed that I refused to consider handing the business over to you. But I thought you accepted it, Antonia. I trusted you to act with integrity. To honour the contract made——'

'Ray, please... what's this all about?' she cried in bewilderment. He had never been so angry with her... never in all her life!

'Don't pretend you don't know, Antonia!' His hands jabbed at the air impatiently. 'Today I lunched with Harry Jessop. He was delighted to tell me how you persuaded him that he needed David Cahill back on the transport company staff to look after his interests. And how he demanded it of Noah Seton. And he cited other instances of your activities...' Ray's face reddened with fury. 'Activities that are in flagrant breach of the contractual agreement I made with Noah Seton. Although, thank God, Harry Jessop didn't know that! I had to sit there with a smile on my face while he told me of the nails that you—my own stepdaughter—have driven into my coffin in every legal and moral sense there is!'

The blood drained from Toni's face.

'You have given Noah Seton every justification to take me to court for damages that could bleed me of every cent I own!' Ray hammered at her. 'He can get me for malicious damage and...' His mouth closed into a pained grimace, and he shook his head as if he couldn't bear to think about the consequences of her actions.

'I... I never read the contract between you.' It was no excuse and Toni knew it. Yet she would never have put Ray in this awful jeopardy if she had known. Never! Not for the sake of twenty-seven people or all the other people in the world! She sank down on the nearest chair, her legs too wobbly to support her. 'I'm sorry... I'm sorry...' she whispered, too shocked to say anything else.

'It's not the money. It's the shame of it!' Ray cried in bitter anguish. 'My reputation. I have always dealt with integrity. Always...my word...my bond. Surely to God you knew that good will is automatically tied to take-overs, Antonia?'

All the despair in the world seemed to be embodied in her name. Toni bowed her head in wretched guilt, miserably aware that there was nothing she could do or say to mitigate her offence or wipe it away.

It suddenly dawned on her what Noah Seton had had up his sleeve this afternoon...the power to crush...any time he chose! Had she incriminated herself and Ray further by accepting the settlement that he had agreed to...all too easily? Was it a case of giving her enough rope to make the hanging an inevitable result?

'No wonder Noah hasn't been in touch with either me or Jocelyn all week!' Ray muttered, the impassioned indictment of a few moments ago sinking into limp defeat.

'He came to my office this afternoon,' Toni blurted out, driven to confess the full extent of her damning activities. 'He said he wanted to re-employ the four men whom I...whom I had made it necessary for him to re-employ.' She couldn't look at Ray. She was too ashamed. 'I demanded that he pay them three months' wages as compensation for having been fired, and...and the same amount as commission for myself,' she added in a very small voice.

'My God!' The appalled mutter was worse than a whole tirade of accusation. She heard his sharp intake of breath and lifted her head, frightened that he might be having a heart attack. He met her apprehensive gaze with sickened eyes. 'So, tell me the worst, Antonia. What happened?'

Her cheeks burnt with the memory as she related every detail of the afternoon's encounter with Noah Seton. Well, not quite every detail. She skated over the paint-spot on the nose, which was certainly irrelevant.

Ray shook his head in incredulous relief. 'He's letting us off the hook for Jocelyn's sake. Paying up...not even telling me...letting you get away with it. *Deliberately* letting you get away with it. That's why he hasn't been in touch with me. Unbelievable!'

His eyes stabbed hard at Toni. 'No more! Do you understand me, Antonia? This is the end of your enmity towards Noah Seton! If you so much as——'

'No more, I promise,' Toni rushed in vehemently. 'I'd never do anything to hurt you, Ray. I never meant to...' Tears swam into her eyes.

'Antonia...' he sighed, his anger melting at the tragic face she lifted to him.

'I'm sorry,' she choked out. 'I'll give him back the money. I'll——'

'No!' He took a deep breath and spoke with slowly measured deliberation to make sure she got the message. 'You will not return the money, Antonia. You will not give Noah any indication of being aware of the true situation. He has made this sacrifice for Jocelyn. Let it be so. It's the only thing left to do. The man goes up in stature. I admire him. The only way that the present status of our relationship can be maintained with any dignity is to leave the status quo. Do you understand that?'

'Yes,' she whispered.

'And one other thing. You will come to Noah's country home for the weekend he asked us. You will be a gracious guest. And I *mean* gracious. Courteous to a fault. I've never asked anything of you before, Antonia. I'm asking you now. For what he has swallowed from you, you owe him that and a great deal more. Is that clear?'

'Yes.'

He looked very drawn and weary as he added, 'I can only hope that Jocelyn will meet his expectations. I don't know how we can make it up to him otherwise.'

Toni writhed with even more guilt as she recollected how she had stirred up Richard Gilbert to supplant Noah Seton in Jocelyn's affections...if he could. As much as it pained her, she could only hope he hadn't succeeded. If Noah didn't get Jocelyn ... after all this ... She closed her eyes, swaying slightly as a wave of faintness swept through her.

A hand grasped her shoulder, squeezing gently, apologetically. His voice floated over her in gruff kindness. 'I've been hard on you. I'm sorry, my dear. All the worry...my own fault really. I should have remembered how passionately you feel things. How you throw yourself whole-heartedly into your crusades. If I'd taken more notice of what you were up to...'

'It's all my fault, Ray.' She looked up at him with swimming eyes, begging his forgiveness. 'I didn't mean to do it. I've spoilt your retirement and...and I meant to be kind...and considerate...and not cost you anything.'

He gathered her up in his arms and tenderly stroked her hair as she sobbed out her pent-up distress.

'Perhaps...if I disappear...'

'Hush, my dear,' Ray soothed. 'It'll work out all right. Somehow.' Always swinging from one extreme to the other, he thought, blaming himself severely for his lack of foresight. He tilted back her head and gave her a lop-sided smile. 'I'd sooner be bankrupted than never see you again, Antonia. Now dry your tears...there's a good girl.' He offered her his handkerchief as he had done a thousand times before.

Toni mopped up her face and blew her nose, but there was no real consolation in his words...only his love, which she didn't deserve one bit. But she would make it up to him. And, if it came to the crunch, she wouldn't let Ray shoulder the responsibility for her idiocy.

Suddenly, what Noah Seton wanted out of life was becoming very important to her.

CHAPTER SEVEN

TONI spent most of Saturday settling Mr Templeton where she wanted him. It helped take her mind off other less happy things. All in all, her plan to get him placed with Lillian Devereux went off without a hitch. He was charmed by the gracious lady, and Lillian positively bridled with feminine pleasure at his courtly manners. For the time being, the idea of men as pigs was completely forgotten.

Toni foresaw no problems with involving him in the auction scheme as time went on. Lillian was very responsive to coaching. It was simply a matter of feeding her the appropriate lines. Toni just hoped that all Mr Templeton's cooking was as good as his tuna soufflé.

As much as she would have liked to forget that Noah Seton was far from being a pig, she couldn't. It preyed on her conscience that she had been so mean about him while all the time he had been nothing but generous. Although he *had* taken that kiss...and she still found it difficult to reconcile that with his supposed commitment to Jocelyn. Some things just didn't add up. Although they undoubtedly did to him with his calculator mind. And his ninety-two per cent!

Nevertheless, no matter what she thought or felt about him, her own course was clear. As spelled out by Ray. She would do exactly as he said. She would not let her stepfather down again. Not in any shape or form.

However, when she saw her beautiful stepsister getting ready for a date on Saturday night, Toni was torn by conflicting emotions. Was everything proceeding as Noah Seton wished, or was Jocelyn dallying with Richard Gilbert? Driven to know the truth—although neither alternative made her feel good—Toni propped herself in Jocelyn's bedroom doorway and led into the questions she needed answered.

'That looks perfect on you,' she remarked, admiring the peach silk dress that her stepsister was smoothing over her slim hips.

Jocelyn flashed her a smile. 'Thanks, Toni. I fell in love with it this morning and bought it on the spot.'

'Is Noah taking you somewhere special?' Toni managed casually, although she felt dreadfully tense inside.

Jocelyn picked up her hairbrush and began running it through her long silky mane. 'Actually he's away this weekend. Business, he said.' The reply was just as studiedly casual as Toni's question.

Guilt increased the turmoil in Toni's stomach. 'So who are you going out with?' she asked.

'Oh, it's just a party with friends,' Jocelyn tossed out. The hairbrush suddenly stopped. The lovely amber eyes were turned on Toni, but weren't sharply focused. There was a tense look of searching on the usually serene face. 'Toni, are you interested in Noah?'

'Naturally I have some interest in him,' Toni answered carefully. She and Ray had agreed that Jocelyn shouldn't be told the present delicate state of affairs in case she should feel pressured by it. Which wouldn't be fair. Toni forced a smile. 'After all, if you're going to marry——'

'I don't mean that kind of interest.' Jocelyn frowned. 'I mean . . . attracted . . .'

Which was much trickier question. Toni shrugged and answered with a partial truth. 'Not my type.' After all, she much preferred men who scored her at a hundred per cent. 'Why do you ask?'

'Just a thought,' Jocelyn muttered, looking somewhat displeased with the answer. 'You were acting kind of funny the other night when you were asking me about him. I wondered . . . and that walk in the rose-garden . . .'

'I explained that, Jocelyn,' Toni put in sharply.

'Yes. Well . . . it doesn't matter.' She resumed brushing her hair. 'Are you coming with us to his home next weekend?'

'Yes. Ray talked me into it. Family unity and best behaviour. You can count on it,' Toni assured her.

'I'm glad you'll be there.'

Toni wasn't. She hated the very thought of being there. But apparently Jocelyn and Noah were still heading towards marriage and she had to stand by and applaud the match. At least it meant that Ray could rest easy.

She drifted off, deep in dire thought, and tried not to notice any of Jocelyn's comings and goings over the next couple of days. She had enough to worry about . . . such as how to act with Noah Seton when he came to her office on Tuesday. It was all very difficult.

Toni was not given to nerves. She couldn't remember ever feeling nervous about anything, not even on her wedding-day. Which, in hindsight, was a mistake. If her danger receptors had been working right, she should have felt nervous about that.

On the other hand, Noah Seton was an entirely different proposition from Murray Sheldon. He wasn't a criminal, for one thing. At least, it hadn't been proved yet. Another consideration was that her ex-husand had only been endowed with animal cunning. Noah Seton had brains. If she made a slip while talking to him he would put two and two together faster than lightning. This possibility did terrible things to her nerves as the hours on Tuesday slowly passed from morning to afternoon.

She had spent all the previous night choosing a subdued and dignified outfit to wear—nothing sassy like the red dress, and nothing as rattily casual as the pink boiler-suit—and she hoped he would appreciate that subtle change in her. She was satisfied that the emerald-green linen suit was the epitome of class: high necked, beautifully cut to fit her figure snugly, and with a conventionally modest hemline. She was quite sure he wouldn't stare at her so disconcertingly today. She needed everything to be straightforward and businesslike.

It was just after four o'clock when he finally came to her office, knocking before entering this time. Toni leapt up from her chair, anxious to greet him nicely. Somehow her tongue clove to the roof of her mouth and nothing came out. He didn't help at all. He looked at her almost as if he was hungry for the sight of her. Which reason told her was absurd.

Second thoughts suggested he wouldn't mind eating her up and smacking his lips over the tasty meal she would make. Toni's pulse started pumping as if she were racing Griffith-Joyner in a hundred-metre sprint.

'Hello,' she said weakly.

'I trust this isn't an inconvenient time for me to call.'

'No. I've got the books on the truck ready for you. Please . . . sit down.' Her hand fluttered an invitation to the chair she had placed on the other side of her desk.

'Thank you.'

The beige suit he wore seemed to highlight his dark good looks, and Toni found herself revising her view of him. Noah Seton was not nearly as ugly as she had first thought. He was, in fact, becoming strikingly handsome. However, her pleasure in his looks was completely spoiled when he extracted a commercial piece of paper from his pocket and offered it to her.

'The cheque,' he said matter-of-factly. 'I thought, since I was coming here myself, I'd by-pass the postal service.'

It was like taking hold of a deadly snake that was threatening to bite at any second. Toni's hand gave a betraying twitch as she stared down at the damning little bank-slip with all the terrible zeroes on it. A tide of burning shame crept up her neck.

'Something wrong?' Noah Seton asked.

'I . . . I didn't realise how much it would be.' She swallowed hard and lifted deeply troubled green eyes. 'Perhaps I overdid the commission. I'm not very good at money. Strong on ideas, but. . .' She shook her head in bewilderment. 'Why didn't you argue me down?'

'It suited me to pay what you demanded,' he replied, and there was steel in those dark brown eyes.

The sharpest nails in the coffin, Toni realised with a rapidly sinking heart. And he was hammering them into place one by one. This cheque was hard evidence of what she had done. It started burning a hole in her hand. To accept it was like signing her own death warrant.

'I think I was somewhat excessive,' she tried again, her eyes filling with luminous appeal.

The sense of power that emanated from him told her just how hollow her victory had been on Friday. He knew he had control of the situation. It showed in the mocking challenge that glittered back at her.

'Not at all. Don't forget to put it in the bank before you go home.'

Which would doom her completely. Yet she couldn't say any more. That would be against Ray's instructions. 'I'll try to remember,' she muttered, and dropped the cheque into her top desk drawer—out of sight, but not out of mind.

She sat down, more out of necessity than design— her legs had become very shaky—but she covered up any distress signals by pushing the books across to him in obvious invitation.

He sat down and started going through them. The questions about the operation of the courier service kept coming, which helped to focus her concentration on less disturbing matters. Then he subjected her to that devastating grin of his and even her concentration was lost.

'You've proved one thing,' he acknowledged. 'You're certainly strong on ideas. You can make a good business from this. No doubt about it. I recall you saying that you had ideas you wanted to implement at the transport company if Ray had chosen to let you take over.'

'Yes,' she admitted. 'The transport business is just begging to be revolutionised.'

His mouth quirked. 'In what way?'

Toni set out to show him. Giving him some of the fruits of her brainwork was one way of easing her conscience for accepting all that money from him.

'You must know the great strides that TNT and Brambles have taken in Europe and America. But they've missed out on one area. I've seen how you can integrate the railway network in Europe, starting with Germany, so that...'

He listened with flattering interest as she explained her theories and how they could be applied. His eyes glowed with an approval that Toni found quite intoxicating. When she came to the end of her exposition, she wished she had some more great ideas to tell him, but he looked very satisfied with what he had learnt from her.

'I'm beginning to think Ray made a mistake in not letting you have your head,' Noah remarked respectfully. 'But then he's probably right about your remarrying some time in the future.'

Toni scathingly put that judgement on the scrapheap. 'You're living in dreamland! No one will ever convince me to be a wife again,' she stated emphatically.

His eyebrows kicked up. 'Tell me why not. What's wrong with being a wife?'

Toni sliced him a scornful look. 'Love, honour and obey...a girl would have to be daft! Husbands expect you to give in to them on everything. And then they misuse what you do give them. I don't intend to surrender my independence for anyone. I'm free. I'm easy. I go where I like, when I like, how I like, and do what I like. Someone would have to offer me a great deal more than I can imagine to give that up.'

'As I commented before, you chose the wrong partner,' Noah said with maddening complacency. 'With the right person...'

The assessing way he was looking at her...Toni started to get a horrid, trapped feeling. It made her want to blast his argument away, but she suddenly recollected that she shouldn't fight with him. She did her best to shrug off the feeling . . . and the touchy discussion.

'In any event,' she said airily, 'I make a rotten wife. It's not my vocation. I can't cook. I forget to do the laundry. And I wouldn't be good with kids. Definitely not.'

'Why wouldn't you be good with them?' Noah asked curiously.

'I haven't got Jocelyn's unlimited patience. They don't fit into my life. I like having fun. They'd end up running wild. No proper meals. No clean clothes . . .'

'I think you would be good with them. Once you decided to have them,' he added hastily.

Toni looked at him incredulously. 'Didn't you hear me? They're not my scene! I don't get involved with people.'

Noah's mouth curled with dry irony. 'Oh, I wouldn't say that. You made yourself responsible for the future well-being of twenty-seven people. What's the score now?'

'Twelve.' She had manoeuvred another one into a job the day before. 'But that's not the point,' she added testily.

The glitter of secret triumph in his eyes stabbed straight to Toni's heart. He stood up, pointedly bringing their conversation to an end. It forcefully reminded Toni of the control he held. 'I'll look forward to seeing you at the weekend,' he said.

'Noah . . .' Toni scrambled to her feet, anxious to keep him with her until she found out more, although she wasn't at all sure how to go about it. 'This weekend...' she started tentatively. 'Do you really want me there?'

'Oh, yes,' he drawled. 'Most assuredly. Who knows what changes it might make in our lives? There could be one or two announcements we might like to make.'

Toni's stomach misbehaved. 'Are you and Jocelyn going to announce your engagement?' she demanded bluntly, telling herself she would feel better once she knew that matter was settled.

He went very still. 'Why do you think that?'

'Everyone... doesn't everyone think that?'

'I have no idea what *everyone* is thinking. What I am thinking, I don't reveal...until I'm ready.'

He walked out on that exit line, and Toni was left with the strong sensation that the sword of Damocles was hanging over her head, poised to drop at Noah Seton's command. The terrible, trapped kind of feeling increased in strength.

She wilted back on to her chair and set her mind to searching for escape routes. It was impossible to settle on any until she knew what Noah Seton intended to do. Without a doubt he was the trickiest, most devious, most conniving man she had ever met. And how she could feel attracted to him was completely beyond her!

One resolution firmed in Toni's mind. No matter what calculations Noah Seton had made, she was not going to let him hurt Ray. Somehow she would counter whatever moves he had planned. The trick was to find out what announcements he intended to make before he made them. Meanwhile she would report to Ray that nothing had changed since Friday. Everything had gone ahead smoothly...on the surface.

Since there was no point in stewing over things she couldn't control—as yet—Toni got on with what was

within her control. By Friday she had found good jobs
for four more people, which brought her down to eight
still to be settled.

She had been in touch with Lillian, who was full
of superlatives about Mr Templeton's cooking, and
voiced no complaints at all about having him in her
household. Quite the contrary, they were proving to
be exceptionally compatible. Toni couldn't help
preening herself a bit on that score. The more she
thought about it, the more she reckoned that Lillian
and Mr Templeton were made for each other.

The date for the auction was fixed for two months
ahead, with the ballroom at the Regent Hotel having
been booked for the occasion. Lillian had rallied all
her charity committee members to the cause. They
had listed a marvellous lot of fantasies and were quite
sure they could get them all donated. So much better
than refrigerators, Toni thought delightedly.

Invitations for the auction were being printed and
would be sent out next week. To fit in with that
schedule, Toni set up the necessary luncheon date with
her gossip columnist friend—spadework was essential
to this enterprise—and at Friday noon she locked up
the office, having allocated the rest of the afternoon
to achieving the game-plan.

Diana Goldbach was not at all averse to joining
Toni Braden for a free luncheon. Toni invariably gave
her good copy, and Diana was a born gossip who rel-
ished her power in print. She had made society figures
and broken them—in direct relation to how friendly
they were to her—but Toni Braden was a special case.
She could make things happen, and Diana respected
this ability. It was rare. And it was always good copy—
well worth her time and her friendship.

The two women smiled at each other across their table at Kable's, the premier restaurant at the Regent Hotel. Diana Goldbach was almost twice Toni's age, though no one would know it to look at her. Despite being thrice divorced, she looked no older than her mid-thirties—blonde, svelte, dressed like a fashion model, and with a mind as sharp as razor-blades. Toni considered her the perfect ally.

'I need your help, Diana,' she stated bluntly. 'In return, you'll have the most marvellous fun of your life.'

Diana Goldbach gleamed with anticipation. 'Tell me.'

Toni did so, embellishing the scheme with all her usual vivacity. Diana laughed so much that she was in danger of the most dreadful indigestion.

'I love it!' she declared. 'Now just let me get it straight. What you want is...'

'Nothing that is slanderous, libellous or suable,' Toni warned. 'What we need is cutting, spiteful malice.'

'Got it!' Diana grinned.

'That will get everyone edgy. We want egos on the line. People who have a point to make about their cash flow and bank accounts...'

'Piece of cake!'

'We've got to stir that competitive spirit so they all want to be seen as winners.'

'Leave it to me, my dear. It's as good as done. In fact, they may very well rename this auction—in years to come—the "Night of the Big Spenders".'

'"Tycoons' Bloodbath,"' Toni corrected her.

Diana suffered another paroxysm of laughter and, indeed, had recurring fits of it long after Toni had left.

However, the idea of the auction was no longer new to Toni, and the fun of it was quickly overshadowed by more immediate circumstances. The weekend was virtually upon her, and tomorrow she had to face Noah Seton again. That was not going to be easy with Ray and Jocelyn in close attendance.

As though things weren't complicated enough, Toni was no sooner home than Jocelyn delivered what could only be called a king-hit!

'You did what?' Toni almost yelled at her stepsister. It started off as a yell, but shock strangled it into a high-pitched squeak.

'I had to!'

Jocelyn wrung her hands. Never in her life had she looked less serene. She paced nervously around Toni's bedroom, her big amber eyes imploring her stepsister's understanding and compliance.

'Please, Toni, I've fallen in love and...it can't matter to you. All I'm asking is that you bring Richard Gilbert as your partner for the weekend. Noah said it was all right with him. It's only until I get the chance to explain to Noah that I've fallen in love with someone else and...and then Richard and I can leave.'

'And then what happens to me and Ray?' Toni demanded, horrified at the thought of a thwarted and humiliated Noah Seton.

'Oh, Toni! You know you can handle anything.' Jocelyn passed it off as if it was nothing! 'Father and Noah have business in common,' she continued, reasoning it all out. 'They respect each other anyway. It won't look so bad with you both staying on there. And Noah isn't in love with me. I'm sure of that. Otherwise I wouldn't do it. Truly I wouldn't.'

'How can you be sure Noah doesn't love you?' Toni demanded in exasperation.

'Because Richard does,' Jocelyn explained.

'One hardly excludes the other!' Toni pointed out acidly.

'I'm not Noah's equal, Toni. It's different with Richard. We're completely in sympathy...' an infuriatingly smug little smile flitted over her lips '...with everything. Richard is a much simpler person than Noah. And he's what I want. Although it is a shame to let Noah Seton get away...' She frowned at Toni. 'One of us should have him. Wouldn't you be interested in——?'

'No!' Toni exploded. 'The last—the very last—way I'd describe Noah Seton is as a parcel to be passed around! He is—very much—his own man.'

Jocelyn sighed. 'Exactly. Noah doesn't need me. Not like Richard.'

'Does Richard Gilbert agree to this...this...' For once in her life, Toni was lost for words.

'Of course! Richard says he'd do anything for me. I'm sure he would. Yet, it's all so terribly awkward. I haven't seen Noah since the party here, and I couldn't tell him over the telephone, could I?'

Awkward would have to be the understatement of the year, Toni thought feverishly.

'So you will bring Richard with you, won't you?' Jocelyn pressed. 'It's all set up. You only have to be Richard's partner for a little while. And I'm definitely going to marry him, Toni, so it will give you the chance to get to know him and——'

'You don't leave me with much choice,' Toni said glumly. Already she could see this weekend shattering into a million irrecoverable pieces.

Jocelyn rushed over and hugged her. 'I knew you wouldn't let me down, Toni.'

What with not letting Jocelyn down, and not letting Ray down, Toni couldn't see any way at all of not letting Noah Seton down.

She supposed she could try to seduce him.

But that hardly carried any credibility if she had Richard Gilbert in tow. And it wasn't as if it was a hundred per cent certainty anyway. Not when Noah only scored her at ninety-two.

No doubt about it—she was looking down the gun barrel of disaster!

CHAPTER EIGHT

THE next morning did not shine brightly. The lowering sky was a portent of thunderstorms ahead. Toni decided to eat a good breakfast. She had the feeling that it might be the last meal she would ever enjoy. Besides which, it meant that she would at least leave Mrs Frobisher feeling pleased and appreciated.

While she was at the table she consulted the horoscopes in the newspaper. Toni did not really believe in astrology—not in any hard-core sense—but at this crucial stage in her life she was not taking any chances on anything. She needed all the backing she could get.

The omens were not good. Her star-sign read, 'Today should bring lots of variety, new interests, contacts, decisions, plans, outings. Any of these could be unusual or complicated. Don't invite trouble or bring something to an end unless you have something better to replace it with. Good fortune can come in many different ways.'

'Something better to replace it with'—there was the rub! She couldn't replace the money or the good will, and when Noah Seton lost Jocelyn too... Gloom clouded Toni's mind. The last thing she wanted was to invite trouble. The trick was to find a way to get out of it!

'Jocelyn tells me you're not coming with us in the car, Antonia,' Ray commented as Toni put the newspaper down.

She looked up to find a worrisome frown on his genial face. Toni shot a telling look at Jocelyn, who had assumed an expression of bland innocence. 'I hope Jocelyn also told you it was her idea for me to bring a friend. To even up the party.' There was a limit to fighting her stepsister's battles for her!

'Noah did approve, Dad,' Jocelyn said, as though butter wouldn't melt in her mouth.

Ray's face didn't completely clear. 'Who is this Richard Gilbert, Antonia? Have I met him?'

Clearly Jocelyn had not been as direct with her father as she had been with Toni. Perhaps she did not want Ray upset or disturbed, and hoped it could be avoided altogether. There was not much chance of that, Toni thought, but she rose to the occasion once more. Habit died hard. She had fought so many battles on behalf of her stepsister. This was just another along the way.

'He was at our party, Ray. You must have been introduced. He's a doctor at the hospital where Jocelyn works. And he was kind enough to put some business my way...'

She went on to explain about the medical courier service and how Noah Seton had judged it to be an excellent business prospect. Ray was all smiles by the time she finished. Toni was left feeling she had dug another foot to her own grave. What she needed was a miracle. Probably half a dozen miracles. She wondered if God was looking her way today, and sent up a prayer just in case.

Ray and Jocelyn had already left when the good doctor arrived to pick up Toni. He drove a BMW, so Toni figured he wasn't exactly on the poverty line, but that didn't make her look at him any less sourly. It wasn't as if she minded him marrying Jocelyn—he

really was far better suited to her stepsister than Noah
Seton—but he could have got his timing a lot better.
The fact that she herself had stirred him into more
positive action did not mitigate that offence at all.

To cap it off, she had to listen to him extolling
Jocelyn's virtues for the whole two-hour trip down to
Bowral. And accept his gratitude for being so co-
operative about this weekend. All in all, to Toni, the
festive mood for this party was sadly lacking. In fact,
it took on the appearance of a time bomb about to
go out of control. If it wasn't out of control already!

To Toni's private amazement, the sky cleared as
they approached their destination, and the sun was
actually beaming down at them as Richard turned his
car into the gateway of Noah Seton's country home.
'Summerfield Green', it was called, according to the
brass plate set in the high brick wall.

Certainly the lawns were very green, Toni conceded
as they proceeded slowly along the curved driveway.
Her gloom lifted. No one with any soul could retain
gloom in the face of the beauty that some gifted hand
had created to set off Noah Seton's home.
The trees were all magnificent specimens. The garden-
beds were ablaze with glorious colour. The driveway
wound under a fabulous wistaria arch as it led to the
front steps of the house. This was a huge white two-
storeyed structure with a porticoed entrance that gave
the façade a charm and grace that one always imagined of the American South.

Toni recollected what Jocelyn had told her about
Noah in her many little confidences. He was from a
wealthy family. He had inherited this particular
property when his parents had died some years ago.
He had one sister who was married to an American,

and they lived near Lexington in Kentucky. To most intents and purposes, Noah was alone in the world, but if he lived in this kind of splendour Toni reckoned that loneliness shouldn't be too hard to take.

She couldn't help thinking that Jocelyn was giving up a lot to marry Richard Gilbert. She felt a woman could not be considered unfortunate if she had to spend her life here. The thought had obviously occurred to the good doctor also. He was frowning rather heavily as he helped Toni out of the car, and his tension regenerated Toni's. The road ahead might be paved with primroses, but it could still lead to hell!

She put a hand on Richard's arm in kindly warning. 'Many strange things could happen here this weekend.'

He nodded gloomily. 'I appreciate that. Only too well.'

Toni sighed. Some people gave up too easily. She had to put some backbone into him. Apart from which, he had to learn to fight Jocelyn's battles for her. Once they were married, Toni wouldn't be around to do it. And, much as it grieved her, she suspected Jocelyn would always need to lean on someone. Her stepsister was not one of the movers and shakers of this world.

'Doctor,' she said sternly, 'everybody gets one chance in life. This weekend is yours—take it. Otherwise you'll regret it all your life. Whatever happens, remember one thing: grab every opportunity. Above all else, you are not to be a wimp.'

His face stiffened up and assumed the expression of determination that the marines had probably worn when they were told they were going to hit the sands of Iwo Jima.

It inspired Toni to a similar determination. While it was almost impossible for Jocelyn to do wrong—

in her eyes—Noah Seton's predicament did excite
feelings of natural sympathy. Toni was resolved to help
him overcome the terrible hurt he would suffer to the
best of her ability. Therefore there was much to
accomplish.

She and Richard were about to mount the steps to
the house when they were hailed from another
direction. Noah Seton, quickly followed by Jocelyn,
broke away from a group of guests who were obviously being given a guided tour around the garden.
Noah walked so fast that Jocelyn almost had to run
to catch up with him, yet the look on her face was
most indiscreet.

Toni hoped that Richard's face didn't reflect the
same love-struck expression. Otherwise there was no
point in Jocelyn's confessing her inconstancy. It would
be obvious to a blind duck! And for Noah that would
be like rubbing salt in the wound.

Fortunately, his gaze was fixed on Toni and she
quickly gave him a force-ten smile in the hope of
keeping his eyes on her. Much to her satisfaction, it
succeeded. Her dress—worn especially for the occasion—also helped to achieve the aim of distracting
him. The vivid yellow and orange sun-dress looked
good aginst her suntan, although she had chosen it
more to boost her low spirits than to attract his
attention.

This was certainly one time she didn't mind him
staring at her. She didn't mind staring at him either.
He was dressed in tropical white shorts and a navy
and white cotton-knit shirt. He was, without a doubt,
an exceptionally sexy male. Toni felt there had to be
something wrong with Jocelyn's chemistry that she
could prefer Richard Gilbert. But . . . it was not hers
to reason why . . . hers but to do or die . . .

Toni would have quite enjoyed quoting her person-
alised version of Tennyson's lines at Noah Seton, but
felt it was inappropriate just now. Besides, she didn't
want him thinking the situation was as bad as it was.
Even if he did think it was as bad as it was, he could
do his worst and she would get around it somehow.

'What a lovely place you have here!' she greeted
him, slipping her arm around his in the friendliest
possible overture. Now was not the time to be
backward in coming forward. Her eyes glowed with
interest as she added, 'Ray was saying that the head
gardener has served you and your parents for over
forty years.'

'Yes. It's his creation as much as anyone else's,' he
replied, his eyes sharply searching hers as though he
was deeply suspicious of her friendliness. But he didn't
seem inclined to let her arm slip away. He hugged it
to his side, trapping it there as he turned to offer a
polite welcome to Richard.

Toni was relieved to see that Jocelyn was now con-
trolling herself. To flaunt her feelings for Richard in
front of Noah would be the height of bad taste. Toni
raised an enquiring eyebrow at her and received a
slight shake of the head and a look of poignant appeal
in response.

No change in the status quo! Noah was still ig-
norant of Jocelyn's defection and Jocelyn wanted her
stepsister's help... 'Once more unto the breach, dear
friends,' Toni quoted to herself. She could match
Noah Seton with Shakespeare any day! However, it
was clear that tactical manoeuvring had to be employed, and that was infinitely trickier with a man
like Noah Seton than simply matching knowledge with
him.

The men greeted each other affably enough. Noah recalled their brief meeting in the rose-garden on the night of the party, then sliced Toni a mocking look that was too full of knowledge for her comfort. He was up to something—and he knew she was up to something—but for the time being he was content to go along with it. Toni smothered a sigh of relief and kept a bright smile fixed on her face.

Noah smoothly suggested they join his other guests on a walk through the garden, and they all set off together. Whether by design or accident, Jocelyn and Richard fell behind, and Noah deliberately steered Toni away from them. He broke off his chat on horticultural matters to make a low, taunting remark.

'I've heard of women who keep making mistake after mistake in their choice of relationships. But I thought you were smarter than that, Toni.'

She gaped up at him, completely taken aback. 'What's wrong with my choice of partners?' she demanded.

His eyes bored into hers, totally uncompromising. 'Obviously your ex-husband has a lot to answer for. It's a matter I want to get to the bottom of. But, whatever happened with him, it's no reason for you to take on a tame pet. You're already bored with Richard Gilbert. Admit it.'

It was as good an opportunity as she would get to put in some effective spadework. Her green eyes sparkled with counter-challenge. 'Of course I am. As you are with Jocelyn. This really is a case of the kettle calling the pot black. We're both tarred with the same brush.'

He paused in his step, that odd stillness coming over him, just as it had on other occasions when they had been talking. Had he been struck by a great truth?

Or had she offended him? Deeply! With Noah Seton it was very difficult to tell. Toni waited, her heart thumping erratically. There was a cautious reserve in his eyes when he eventually spoke.

'Are you saying what I think you're saying, Toni?'

This was a very difficult question to answer. 'I've got no idea,' she replied with some tact, then decided that retreat was not the order of the day. 'All I'm saying is you're no more suited to Jocelyn than I am to Richard. With Jocelyn you're simply ready to settle for a tame wife who's nicely presented and who'll give you the children you want.' She paused, then deliberately threw his own challenge back at him. 'Why don't you admit that?'

A funny little smile flitted over his lips and disappeared. 'Marriage was certainly a consideration at one time,' he mused, but Toni got the distinct impression he was holding something back. 'Although, if I get your meaning correctly,' he continued, 'it would seem that you're not recommending Jocelyn to me as a future bride.'

There was no alternative but to take the bull by the horns. Toni plunged straight in. 'Jocelyn has tremendous virtues. Including her virtue. For the right man she'll make an ideal wife. But for you—let's be quite frank—you'll be bored out of your mind within six months. I've been through the mill. I know,' she declared with firm authority.

A lively interest sparkled into Noah Seton's eyes. He seemed to like the way in which this conversation was moving. 'Then you would recommend someone— shall we say—more adventurous?' he asked in a tone that clearly indicated he was not offended. In fact, he sounded fascianted.

'Definitely!' Toni approved.

'Someone . . . more challenging . . . unpredictable . . . charismatic . . .'

He was obviously warming to the idea and Toni helped him along. 'That's what you need. Someone who'll always excite your interest.'

'I see,' he murmured, then after a thoughtful pause—which Toni allowed him in order for these truths to sink in—he seemed to come to a decision.

'I think you're right about that. Very astute of you. You are aware . . .' he added carefully, as if picking his way over slippery stepping-stones in the middle of a fast-running brook. 'You are aware that I am not in love with Jocelyn?'

'How could I be aware of that?' Toni said with considerable haughtiness. 'As you told me yourself, you reveal nothing until you are ready.' He deserved that shot for all the heartache he had given her over his kiss, Toni thought, but she instantly rethreaded the line towards her stepsister's freedom. 'Jocelyn, however, was well aware of a lack of ardour . . .'

'Are her feelings hurt?' he asked with a satisfying show of concern. It demonstrated that he had some humanity along with that computer brain.

'Not at all,' Toni returned airily, letting him completely off the hook. 'It meant nothing to her. The merest trifle . . .'

Noah seemed to be having trouble with his mouth. Perhaps the twitching was a sign of relief. He compressed his lips hard, took a deep breath, and slowly put forward a supposition. 'If her affections were now otherwise engaged . . . with someone who would never find her boring . . . someone with whom she shared interests in common . . .'

He paused and glanced back to where Jocelyn and Richard were halted beside a splendid copper beech tree, although they looked more involved with each other than intent on admiring the leafy boughs.

'Someone...perhaps...like Dr Richard Gilbert...' the brilliantly perceptive dark eyes came slicing back to Toni; one eyebrow rose in conspiratorial enquiry '...who works at the same hospital...and appears to be...very companionable with her at the moment.'

'A likely match,' Toni agreed, without so much as a flutter of an eyelash. 'I'm sure they could be very compatible. It would probably be a kindness for us to withdraw any separate claims we have on their time. And, of course, that would leave you free and unencumbered...'

'...to look for someone who would make certain my life was never boring.'

'Exactly!'

'That certainly appeals to me,' he approved. 'You're quite sure there would be no hurt involved if we— er—leave Jocelyn and Richard to their own pursuit of harmony and happiness?'

'Absolutely certain,' Toni assured him.

'Ah!' he breathed, on a long-drawn-out sigh of satisfaction.

Toni smiled, elated that he had understood her so well. And she had managed it all without giving any hurt to his ego. In fact, his eyes danced back at her with more than gratitude. They definitely held a gleam of unholy joy.

'Please accept my apology for what I said earlier,' he said handsomely. 'You are an exceptionally smart woman, Toni Braden. And, now that I think about it, I've never yet found you boring.'

Her bloodstream overheated in a most embarrassing fashion. It had not occurred to Toni that Noah would interpret her advice as pushing herself as a candidate for his attentions. She suddenly realised that it might have sounded that she was eager to supplant Jocelyn in his affections. Which was not the truth at all!

Never in a million years would she have interfered if Jocelyn had truly been in love with him. She had only egged Richard on a little because Jocelyn had seemed piqued by the good doctor's failure to commit himself when faced with Noah. If it hadn't worked out she would have stuck by her principles of non-interference in other people's relationships.

'Noah...' It was on the tip of her tongue to tell him he had misunderstood her motives, but she found herself treacherously responding to the warm wickedness in his eyes. There was...a certain piquancy...to the challenge he was projecting. And no one else had ever excited her so much with a mere kiss. Surely there was no harm in playing along with him...for a little while? 'I accept your apology,' she finished graciously.

His grin rattled all her reservations about allowing a man into her life. Noah Seton was different from other men. Apart from the way he could kiss, he had the kind of mind that she was beginning to admire. Computers weren't all bad. One couldn't criticise their logic. It was impeccable. And logic could be very satisfying sometimes.

'How pleasant it is to find us in agreement for once!' he said in a low, purring tone that seemed to stroke all over Toni's skin. He drew her arm more intimately around his and set forth again on the pathway through the trees. 'There's a lot more of the garden that I want to show you.'

As much as Toni was tempted by his offer, she was not one to postpone responsibility. Jocelyn would be anxious to know if the situation had been resolved favourably, and she couldn't just let her hang in uncertainty. Besides, common sense urged that she needed time to consider her own position with Noah Seton. She had plunged herself into enough trouble already, rushing blindly ahead in her mission to look after the people he had fired. Better to look before she leapt where he was concerned.

'I would love to see everything, Noah,' she said quite truthfully, 'but could we leave it for later on in the day? It might seem rude...to Jocelyn and Richard...if we just go off together right now. And there are your other guests...'

'How remiss of me!' he said glibly. 'I find your company so enthralling, I even forget my duties as host. Later, then,' he agreed, his eyes glittering in a way that gave Toni that trapped feeling again.

She had the weird sensation that everything she had said and done was precisely to his own private purpose. Almost as if he had guided her there. Which was crazy! She had done the guiding! A little too far, probably, but he had certainly not been the one in control of the conversation. He hadn't known what she had known. Yet he had caught on very quickly...

No doubt about it, he was an extremely tricky man! And she wasn't at all sure she should pursue this attraction she felt towards him. Every instinct warned her she would be moving into dangerous territory. On the other hand, she had never been a coward, and, since she wanted to explore it further, why should she deny herself? Apart from all that, it behove her not to alienate the man, particularly since he could hurt Ray if he chose to.

This last reason made Toni feel quite virtuous about her decision. In fact, she was in brimming spirits when

Noah smoothly collected Richard and Jocelyn back into their company and then rounded up the other wandering guests to lead them to the outside entertainment area.

Ray looked somewhat bemused by the odd coupling—Jocelyn with Richard, Toni with Noah, who had kept firm possession of her arm. Toni gave her stepfather a bright reassuring smile, but it was clear that some explanations would be due fairly soon—the way things were going. However, Jocelyn was her first consideration.

The lovely amber eyes kept darting apprehensive glances at her. It was impossible to say anything in front of Noah, but Toni managed to flash her stepsister a 'V for Victory' sign when he wasn't looking. Jocelyn's eyebrows rose in astonishment. A strategy meeting was obviously urgent.

Noah ushered everyone through a magnificent set of wrought-iron gates—seventeenth-century Italian, he informed Toni with a touch of pride. He seemed pleased that she admired them so much. In fact, he looked very pleased with his world at the moment, not the slightest bit grim or steely. It was amazing how much more handsome he was, here on his home territory.

Beyond the gates, vine-covered and latticed pergolas ran around three sides of a swimming-pool and spa, providing ample shade and protection for the large party of people—some thirty guests in all, Toni estimated.

The sparkling green pool had a touch of Tuscany, set off by huge concrete slabs in a dusky salmon-pink colour and large urns full of massed petunias. Toni could not help thinking that Noah Seton had every justification for feeling proud of his home. If it were hers, she would certainly feel proud of it. Indeed, she was so entranced by the scene in front of her that she momentarily forgot her priorities.

Jocelyn put in a timely reminder. 'I think I'll need some sun-screen lotion. Will you excuse me for a few moments, Noah?' she said prettily, then smiled invitingly at Toni. 'Would you like to freshen up, Toni?'

They effected a graceful withdrawal and Jocelyn steered Toni into the house and upstairs to the room she had been given. 'How did you do it?' she demanded, the moment the door was closed behind them.

'With considerable difficulty.' Toni eyed her stepsister sternly. 'This is never to happen again, Jocelyn.'

'I'm certain it won't!' came the hasty promise, but not even Toni's remonstration could quench her delight. 'Richard is nerving himself up to propose. I can feel it. Was Noah . . . terribly upset?'

Toni thought the lesson needed to be rammed home. Jocelyn had to learn to face up to the consequences of her actions, and it was obvious that she was not concentrating well at all. 'Under the circumstances, he took it rather well. I'm doing the best I can to soften the impact of this shattering experience——'

'Oh, thank you, Toni,' Jocelyn breathed, her eyes suddenly brimming. She threw her arms around her smaller but infinitely tougher stepsister and hugged her with excessive emotion. 'Thank you, thank you, thank you. You've always been the most marvellous sister to me. I don't know how I can ever repay you for all you've done over the years. And now this . . .'

Toni sighed heavily, relieving the choked feeling that had clutched her throat. 'You've already repaid me many times over, Jocelyn. Just by being you.'

'Oh, Toni...' She pulled back a little, her face glowing with happiness through her tears. 'That's a lovely thing to say. But I haven't——'

'Don't you start putting yourself down,' Toni warned with gruff fierceness. 'We finished that years ago, remember?'

'Yes, Toni,' she agreed with a wobbly smile.

'Now dry those tears, fix up your face, and be happy with your Richard. I'll take care of Noah Seton.'

'I know it's expecting an awful lot of you, Toni...'

'No trouble at all,' Toni denied blithely. 'I'm liking him better all the time. I intend to enjoy myself immensely.'

Jocelyn laughed in relief and went off to the en-suite bathroom to start following Toni's instructions.

Toni smiled contentedly to herself as she sat down on the bed to wait for her stepsister. We all have different abilities, she thought. Jocelyn had fought so hard to overcome the stutter that had proved so embarrassing and restricting years before. Her patience and application had been truly awesome, and now she spoke beautifully. As she had been through such a painful and trying experience, it was no wonder she was so gifted in dealing with disadvantaged children who were stuck in hospital for weeks and months at a time with chronic illnesses.

Her stepsister was a wonderful person in her own right. She could do a lot of things that Toni couldn't. Apart from being great with children, she could cook and look after housework and was always able to find things. And she was sweet and loving and always believed the best of people...

Toni chided herself for having been impatient and critical with her over this affair with Noah Seton. She could well understand Jocelyn's being somewhat lost with him. He was a very complex person. She felt a bit lost herself. But one thing Toni knew she was good at—dealing effectively with concepts and ideas. That was her strength.

Which brought her back to the problem of Noah Seton. If she dismissed everything else and came right down to the basics, he was simply a man who found her attractive...and her company stimulating. Which was perfectly reasonable. She could handle that. And she certainly wouldn't mind trying out another kiss or two, just to see if that first one was as fantastic as she remembered. In fact, it would give her a lot of pleasure to make him admit that ninety-two per cent was a most erroneous assessment.

Therefore, there was no problem about strolling around the gardens with him. It should prove to be...quite stimulating. And, with a little encouragement on her part, Noah Seton could find himself too compromised to ever pursue a damages case over that good-will business.

A smile of sweet satisfaction spread across Toni's face. The day which had seemed so gloomy this morning was shining up beautifully. Jocelyn was home-free with her Richard. Ray's troubles were almost certainly over. And Noah Seton...well, it was quite true that she was liking him better all the time. The only question was—where would it all end?

CHAPTER NINE

IT BECAME instantly apparent to Toni that, while she and Jocelyn had been having their private conversation in the house, Noah Seton had taken the opportunity to ply Richard Gilbert with every encouragement to follow any inclinations he had towards Jocelyn. The look on the good doctor's face when she and Jocelyn emerged from the house was a clear indication of how successful he had been. Richard Gilbert gave the appearance of a man ready to take on anybody in order to pursue his happiness.

Toni wondered if Jocelyn had cleared her face of the look of rapturous freedom that had been glowing from it, but she didn't give the matter a lot of consideration. Noah slid her a grin that shattered any disciplined train of thought. Toni vaguely picked up nuances of amusement and elation from it, but there were also admiration and a strong dash of challenging anticipation which raised her pulse-rate to a previously unknown tempo of excitement.

Perhaps it was the extra spice of knowing that treading any path with this man could be dangerous. Undoubtedly there were hidden depths to Noah Seton. But Toni didn't pause to examine her feelings. The challenge danced in front of her—drawing her on . . . irresistible!

Noah casually claimed her arm again—almost as if it were a matter of course now—and steered her around the poolside, introducing her to all the guests in a subtly possessive manner which had everyone looking at her with speculative interest. Toni responded with her own speculative interest.

Most of the people lived locally and were perfect illustrations of the old wealth in the district. They wore designer clothes and projected the kind of confidence that came with inbred knowledge of their privileged status. Toni made a mental note to collect names. If any of them were worthy candidates for the auction, Lillian would need to send out more invitations. Certainly they all seemed friendly with Noah Seton, which had to be some recommendation.

While she herself had no objection to Noah's behaviour towards her, Toni noticed that Ray was observing them with a steadily deepening frown. Jocelyn and Richard had dropped out of the introductory socialising early on in the procedure, and were deep in their own private world at one of the smaller tables around the pool. It was patently obvious that Noah wasn't troubled by this desertion, but Ray was too disturbed to let things lie.

Toni felt it was a little unfair of Ray to zero in on her as the linchpin of this particular development. He should have approached Jocelyn, who was more easily accessible than herself at the moment. Apart from which, she herself was perfectly innocent of any wrongdoing this time. However, when he insisted on drawing her aside for a private word, and Noah courteously deferred to Ray's need, Toni resigned herself to shouldering responsibility once again.

'Antonia...' There was a touch of hurt bewilderment in his voice. 'I don't understand...it's not like you to——'

'There's nothing to worry about, Ray,' she assured him gently. 'Jocelyn and Richard are madly in love with each other and they need someone to run interference for them. I'm doing that. And you've got to admit—Noah Seton doesn't look as if he's suffering, does he?'

A range of expressions warred across Ray's face. He looked at Jocelyn. He looked at Noah. He finally looked back at Toni. 'But you don't like him,' he said in a strangled voice. 'Antonia...you can't meddle with a man's dignity. Not Noah Seton's...'

'I promise you, Ray, everything's under control...' Not quite, she amended silently. Her stomach was doing curious things every time Noah's eyes met hers. But that wasn't the point. 'As I told Jocelyn, I'm liking Noah better all the time,' she added with convincing fervour. 'So I'm not really meddling. What I'm doing is replacing what he thought he had with something he thinks is better. And who's to say it isn't? I'm beginning to think it might be the best thing of all.'

'Antonia...' Ray was beginning to look somewhat dazed.

'Ray, I've discovered that the only certain thing in this world is that there isn't any real certainty about anything,' she said firmly. 'Only possibilities and probabilities that have to be worked on. Now, as far as I can see at the moment, everything's fine. So please stop worrying.'

She planted a reassuring kiss on his cheek to ease the strain of readjustment, gave him a cheer-up smile, then turned him back to the group where Noah was holding court. True to the form he had been demonstrating ever since she had taken the first initiative, Noah took her hand to draw her to his side. To Toni's mind, he was clearly inviting any meddling she cared to continue with.

Ray shook his head in total bemusement, then wandered back to his own little party of contemporaries. He sat down, feeling as though he had been hit by a runaway train. But that was not a new experience where Antonia was concerned.

He took a glass of champagne from the tray of a solicitous waiter and sipped at it, letting the relaxing bubbles rise to his brain. Jocelyn looked very happy with Richard Gilbert. Noah Seton looked ... satisfied ... with what was happening.

As Ray had learnt over the years, there was only one way to deal with a runaway train. That was to ride along with it until it stopped of its own accord. And the champagne was exceptionally good. He reflected—with considerable satisfaction—that Noah Seton could well afford to indulge his interest in Antonia.

Eventually an elaborate barbecue luncheon was served. Toni and Noah sat with Jocelyn and Richard, and good will was promoted in every direction. Toni decided that the good doctor would make a remarkably pleasant stepbrother-in-law. However, to her mind, he was no real match for Noah. *Her* Noah, she thought to herself.

As soon as the meal was over Noah stood up and held out his hand to Toni, his eyes intently bright with purpose. 'You were kind enough to show me your mother's roses, Toni. I think it's time I showed you my mother's garden,' he said with deliberation. 'It has some elements that I'm sure will have special appeal to you.'

Naturally, neither Jocelyn or Richard offered any objection to being deserted, and Toni had no compunction at all about leaving them or going with Noah. In fact, she felt exhilarated at the prospect of being alone with him. Perhaps the champagne she had drunk over luncheon had made her feel a little wild and bubbly, but she couldn't entirely discount the effect Noah Seton's close presence had on her. She became more aware of it as they left the party behind.

She had the sense of embarking on a marvellous secret game. Perhaps it was the element of danger that made it all so heady. Whatever... Toni felt intensely alive. Her hand rested on Noah's bare forearm and the soft hairs on his skin made her skin prickle with excitement at the thought of being closer to him.

He played the guide with consummate ease: taking her through the cherry-blossom walkway, pointing out the wistaria umbrella tree, telling her the histories of some of the camellia trees—planted to commemorate various family anniversaries. Eventually they arrived at a high hedge and Noah led her to a door in the centre of it.

'This was my mother's secret garden,' he explained, unlocking the door and ushering Toni into the private enclosure.

Down the centre of the long rectangle surrounded by the hedge was a formally constructed pond. Bordering it on either side were row upon row of standard roses, all in shades of pink. At the end was a lovely white gazebo over which trailed climbing roses, echoing the pink once again. As Toni stepped forward, utterly entranced by the scene in front of her, she saw a flash of gold in the water. She moved closer to watch the magical splendour of tropical fish darting through the pond in their brilliant array of colours.

Delight illuminated her face as she swung around to Noah, who had paused to close the door behind them. 'What a wonderful idea!' she cried. 'What a marvellous retreat from the world!'

'Yes. Completely private,' he said quietly, a look of supreme satisfaction on his face as he strolled towards her.

His intention was crystal-clear to Toni, and she had no wish to postpone the moment she had been waiting for all afternoon. Excitement enlivened her nerve-ends as he slid his arms around her waist. He held her in a loose embrace, his desire kept deliberately in check while his eyes held hers in seductive challenge.

Toni was not about to back down . . . or away. Her hands slithered up over the powerful muscles of his chest. It felt good. It felt right.

'Do you like it here?' His voice was husky, as if her touch had strained his breathing.

Toni didn't know whether he meant being in the garden or being in his arms. 'Yes,' she said.

He nestled her closer. His cheek brushed softly across her temples. A long, warm sigh whispered through the unruly ringlets of her hair. *Sensitive,* Toni thought. Her skin quivered in delight as deliciously dreamy fingertips ran across the top of her shoulders and explored their way down the deep V at the back of her skimpy bodice. Toni was suddenly very glad she had worn this bra-less sun-dress. She felt, rather than heard, the slight expulsion of breath as she leaned against him, slowly moulding the fullness of her breasts to the firm pectoral muscles that her hands had found earlier. It felt more than good. Superlatively right.

His hands slid up to an erotic point beneath the underswell of her breasts, lingering there when her body gave a convulsive little shudder of pleasure. His lips grazed across her forehead, over her eyelids, down to her ears, imprinting gentle little kisses that told her how exquisitely feminine he found her. They moved slowly over her own lips, making sensual arabesque shapes, moulding and remoulding, pliable, supple, persuasive. Toni was totally entranced with what he was doing. Her mind flooded with the image of him kissing her all over ... just like this ... and the desire for him to do so spread like wildfire through her veins.

Her fingers undid the top buttons of his shirt, picked their way over the sparse curly hair below his throat, then slid to the smooth strength of his shoulders. An involuntary tremor shook his body. His mouth suddenly hungered over hers, powered by impulses that went too deep to contain. The new compelling thrust of his kiss tore restraint into meaningless shreds, seductive persuasion splintering into driving possession, sensuality exploding into raw passion. His hands dropped to her hips, pulling her into more provocative contact with him, inflaming the need that vibrated through both of them.

Her fingers climbed up the back of his neck, clutching blindly as their mouths fused in a wild craving for deeper intimacy. Her breasts ached with longing for his touch. She could feel the urgency of his excitement through the thinness of her dress, and strained even closer in exultant response.

A low, guttural sound broke from Noah's throat as he wrenched his mouth from hers. In a whirl of movement that left Toni dizzy and breathless, he swept her off her feet and set off down the line of roses, his arms crushing her against his heaving chest as his long, powerful legs strode the distance to the gazebo. She felt his heart thumping as madly as hers, saw the feverish glitter of purpose in his eyes, heard the harsh rasp of his breath, and knew he urgently wanted to finish what they had started this time.

She had never felt so excited in her life. Inside the gazebo there was a large circular lounging couch, but at the last second Noah seemed to hesitate over laying her down on it. He half swung away, inhaled deeply, then set her feet on the floor beside it. Inexplicably he moved back a pace, his hands spanning her waist, forcibly holding her away from him. Every line of his face was strained from the control he was fighting to attain. His eyes were dark pools of raging turbulence.

'I'm mad...' The words rasped from his lips, gravelled with the conflicting pressures of rampant desire and ingrained self-discipline. 'I only planned to——'

'I want you...' The cry burst from her, totally uncaring of any consequences. She didn't want him planning or calculating anything, and she couldn't bear for him to retreat from her again, to leave her not knowing...

She snatched one of his hands from her waist. Slowly she lifted it. As she spread it over the soft fullness of one of her breasts and held it cradled there, her heart leapt its wild approval. Her eyes recklessly defied him to deny that it was what he wanted too. Everything within her rebelled against his struggle for control, and the urge to break him to her will was like a mad fever through her brain.

His fingers moved, irresistibly drawn to the bare swell of cleavage which was so invitingly delineated by the low halter neckline of her dress. 'Toni...' It was a sibilant cry of need.

'I want you to,' she told him unequivocally, and reached up to untie the fastening of the strap at the back of her neck, obsessively intent on having her own shrieking desires satisfied. She did not care that he might think her brazen or wanton. That was totally irrelevant. She wanted him totally out of control, caught up in a moment they would both remember for the rest of their lives.

Any last wisp of rational decision-making slipped from Noah's mind as he was offered the chance of peeling the ends of her bodice away from the incredibly lush femininity of her breasts. He couldn't stop himself from doing it . . . from filling his hands with the soft, yielding loveliness that was so uninhibitedly presented to him. She was so vibrantly beautiful, so bewitchingly tempting in the proud flaunting of her sexuality.

The touch of her . . . like warm satin quivering with intoxicating life. His whole body screamed with the need to feel all of her in every way possible, to taste the taut brown peaks of her breasts . . . to draw on all of her inner secret magic . . . to know with absolute totality all there was to know . . . to take her now! He couldn't wait . . . couldn't restrain himself . . . no matter what the consequences were or where it led.

Her hands lifted the hem of his basque shirt. Impatience ripped through him. In one quick violent movement he pulled the shirt up over his head and hurled it away. Her laughter was an enticing ripple of exultant excitement. Her body swayed towards him, the tips of her naked breasts brushing the bare skin of his chest as she linked her hands behind his neck. Noah felt the wild release of all care. In his own mad exultation he hoisted her high, needing to take those tantalising peaks in his mouth, wanting to savour all the woman she was, all the femininity she promised.

Toni gasped as Noah's mouth washed over the tingling voluptuousness of her breasts. It was so long since she had been with a man that her nipples ached with need. Her back arched, instinctively offering . . . tempting . . . urging him to take what she so desperately wanted him to. And never before had her need been so excitingly answered. It was magic...sweet torture...exquisite fulfilment...his mouth teasing, provoking, taking each throbbing areola and drawing an intense response which rippled through her entire body.

Her hands clutched at the taut muscles of his shoulders, clawed wild patterns through his thick black hair, clutching him to her in an ecstasy of satisfaction. She moaned his name...this incredible man who could do this...who could make her feel so much...

He lowered her on to soft cushions, slid her clothes away, touched her...his gentle fingers caressing with erotic tenderness, delivering their sensual message of what was to come, building need and want and anticipation into craving, rampant desire. She cried out in mindless protest when he lifted himself away. Her eyes flew to his in wordless eloquent pleading, but the plea was swallowed up by an intense wave of satisfaction as she realised that what he was doing was what she wanted. She could have lain here forever under the magic of kisses and caresses, but she wanted the pleasure of feeling his nakedness against her own...stroking him...kissing him...learning all there was about him.

His eyes looked as black as coals, yet they flamed with intense desire, raking over the voluptuous curves of her body as he stripped away the last of his clothes. He was beautiful, Toni thought, from the rough, springy curls on his chest to the taut calf muscles of his strong legs. The wild disarray of his dark hair and the burning intensity of his eyes gave his face an Odyssean look that made her heart contract with a strange feeling she had never experienced before. He was very special, this man...unique. He was even more magnificent naked than he had been in clothes. And he was hers!

Noah felt he could feast his eyes on Toni forever. She was perfection...the woman he had always been waiting for...wanting... He had never had a woman like her, and he knew with a terrible certainty that there never would be another like her. He was riven by the need to possess and the urge to prolong this incredible experience as long as he could. Yet the chemistry of his body wouldn't let him.

Toni held out her arms and he came to her. The movement of his body against hers was lithe and graceful. She was conscious of herself as a woman in a way she had never been before, as if the man he was brought a new level of sensitivity to her entire being. She loved the feel of him...the touch of him...so strong...so powerful...so intoxicatingly male. She rubbed her thighs against his, slid her hands over the taut muscles of his body, pressed her lips to the throbbing pulse-beat at the base of his throat.

A hoarse cry was driven from his lips and he bent down to take her mouth with his. It was fire and nectar...storm and bliss...and then he was kissing her all over, driving her into a frenzy of need so that Toni barely knew what she was doing...heaving, writhing, quivering in response, clawing at him until at last he gathered her to him, unable to contain himself any longer. He held her poised against him, his eyes seeking hers, pleading, commanding, and the words spilled from his lips, his voice as hoarse as if it had been dragged all the way from limbo.

'I love you, Toni...'

'You don't have to say that,' she cried, shutting her eyes tight as her soul rejected the need for any hypocrisy from him. Not from him. 'You want me...I want you . . . that's all that's necessary.'

'I love you,' he repeated, the words as powerfully driven as his need for her as he thrust himself deeply inside her. He cradled the convulsive little jack-knife of her body, felt the exquisite contraction of her muscles around him, enveloping him, quivering in ecstatic fulfilment at the gathering together of the fluids of life.

'Noah . . .' His name fell from her lips, a whispered acknowledgement, a sigh of blissful satisfaction. He stirred within her and she held him there. She opened her eyes, and in the swimming green pools was a deep fathomless recognition.

Despite the overwrought tension of his body, he paused a moment longer to savour this silent, almost mystical communion . . . an unspeakable knowledge of each other...the sharing of herself with him...the giving . . .

Toni saw the effort he made to hold control, but she had gone beyond that. She ran her fingers down the wonder of his body. The caress drew a paroxysmal spasm that shattered any resolution that had clung to his mind. She tried to match his rhythm, but every movement he made sent a storm of sensation convulsing through her, and her uncontrollable response drove him to a frenzied abandonment of any care but to pound himself so deeply inside her that she would be indelibly stamped with his possession.

She felt his climax as a sweet, melting warmth that permeated her whole body, and when he collapsed on top of her she hugged his crushing weight, her arms and legs entwining the warm solidity of his body with

a fierce possessiveness of her own. All she knew—
and that only on the most primitive level of all—was
that she did not want to be separated from him...ever!

He had reached something in her...touched something...answered something...that no other man
had...and she wanted to keep him as hers for the
rest of her life. He had to be hers. The idea of any
other woman having him was total anathema to her.

How long they stayed locked together was an im-
measurable time of blissful contentment. Even when
Noah moved, he carried her with him as he rolled on
to his back. He began to stroke her hair, softly, tenderly, smoothing the tumbled disarray of wild curls.

Toni drew in a deep breath, determined to seize advantage from any lingering vulnerability he felt towards her. 'If you tell me that was only ninety-two
per cent, Noah, I think I'll kill you.'

She felt him wind a curl around his finger as if he
was considering how best to get his own way. 'If I
said it was beyond measurement...would that please
you?' he asked softly.

'Only if it was the truth.'

'I have no reason to lie this time.'

She heaved herself up. The expression on his face
was more than satisfactory. He looked as if he considered her a mixture of Helen of Troy, Pandora, and
the Sirens of ancient legends who had lured sailors to
their doom.

'So you admit you lied last time?' she demanded
archly.

He grinned, enjoying the intense vivacity of her
face, lit as it was with delighted triumph. 'I did owe
your stepsister some loyalty at that point. I don't now.'

His grin faded as his eyes gathered a purpose that made Toni feel faintly uneasy. It made her recollect that trapped feeling he had given her once or twice before. She wanted him. She harboured no doubt about that. And he wanted her. But nothing ever seemed to work out in a simple, straightforward manner with Noah.

'So we've settled Jocelyn,' she said, feeling her way carefully.

'As far as I was concerned, that matter was settled the moment I saw you,' Noah stated matter-of-factly. 'The rest was only a question of timing.' His mouth curled in light self-mockery. 'Except you have a way of messing up my timing.'

She laughed, elated with her success at having made him lose his formidable control, and tremendously pleased that everything had worked out fortuitously for Jocelyn. She wouldn't have wanted her stepsister hurt. It occurred to her that Noah must have been laughing up his sleeve while she had been talking to him this morning, but that didn't matter now. It thrilled her that he had wanted her all along.

Her eyes sparkled with another lovely realisation. 'Did you do all those things... rehiring some of the employees, and giving me the truck, and paying over all that money...'

He rolled her on to her back and kissed the whole train of thought out of her mind. It took Toni several moments to recollect it when he finally gave her an answer. His eyes bored into hers, as if intent on enforcing his will.

'Yes, I did all those things for you. The only question left is, will you do what I want?'

'And what's that?' she asked distractedly, luxuriating in the sensual way he was moving his body over hers, forcibly reminding her of what they had just shared.

'I want you to marry me, Toni.'

CHAPTER TEN

No... The word screamed through Toni's mind and she barely stopped it exploding off her tongue. She didn't want to hurt Noah, but she had been through this before, and it didn't work. Marriage couldn't work for her. In six months' time ... the end. Noah was confusing sexual need with love. Love was a different thing ... what she felt for Ray ... for Jocelyn ... not this wild, tearing, irresistible response to a person.

She suddenly realised that Noah had gone very still. She had gone still too. She could sense his whole being intensely concentrated on her ... waiting ... wanting ... willing her to say yes.

There was no question in Toni's mind what her answer had to be, but his reaction to her reply was terribly important. This beautiful beginning to the most exciting relationship she had ever had could come to an abrupt end. And she didn't want that. She couldn't bear it. Not now.

Reluctantly she raised her heavy lashes and forced herself to meet the dark intensity of his eyes, her own pleading forgiveness from the innermost depth of her soul. For the first time since she had met him, he looked uncertain ... openly vulnerable. It squeezed her heart. She lifted her hand to tenderly stroke his cheek. The last thing she wanted was to hurt him.

He was paying her one of the highest compliments a man could give a woman. That was how he would think. He was wrong, of course. Given time, he would find that out too. And for a woman it was even worse.

However golden the cage, marriage was a prison for a wife. And she didn't want that. Not again. Never again! She had to be her own person . . . fulfil her own destiny. No matter what he said or promised, it wouldn't work. And everything would be spoiled between them.

'Noah . . .' Her mouth was dry. She swallowed hard and desperately sought for the right words to make him understand. 'What you feel for me . . . what I feel for you . . . it's a totally overwhelming sexual attraction. We both feel it. And it's very special. But it lessens in time. It goes away. Other things affect it. And it becomes . . . not so important. It's no basis for marriage, Noah,' she pleaded. 'I can't marry you for that reason. Eventually you'd become bored with me, and I'd become bored with you.'

'I know what you're saying, Toni,' he said quietly, tenderly stroking the curls away from her temples. His eyes were soft with a reassurance that did dreadful things to her stomach. 'If it were only sexual attraction I felt for you, I wouldn't be asking you to be my wife. I want you always in my life because I love you. Because——'

'Don't say that!' she protested sharply.

'What? That I love you?'

'It's just a word that people use when they want to use other people. Don't do that to me, Noah. I don't ever want to hear it again.'

The vehement passion that had slipped into her voice gave him pause for thought. There was far more to the break-up of her first marriage than a simple issue of incompatibility. The need to tread carefully reached critical mass. Gently . . . knowing intuitively that she might shy away if he erred . . . he felt his way forward.

'Your husband . . . he really hurt you?' he asked softly.

The compassion in his eyes rattled the door to things that Toni had locked away . . . turned her back on. She didn't want to open that door. She had made up her mind to get on with her life, replace negative things with positive things. The hurt was over…finished…cut clean.

There was a sharp, knife-like edge to her voice as she answered the question. Truthfully, but without elaboration. 'Everyone who gets divorced goes through a personal crucifixion, Noah. Unless you've gone through it yourself, you'd never understand.'

He hated the deep reflection of pain and disillusionment in her eyes. He hated the unappreciative fool she had given herself to in marriage. But that didn't help him resolve the problem he knew he had on his hands. If he'd taken more time… Though it was pointless to think about that now. He had to ride the crest of this moment.

He had faced adversity and pain many times before in his life. He cradled her in his arms, instinctively imparting what little comfort she would accept from him. 'I wish I could have saved you that, Toni. I wish we had met sooner,' he said slowly. 'But the future is ours to make what we want of it. And the truth is…I don't care what you do by yourself or for yourself, as long as you share some of yourself with me. For as long as either of us live. Does that sound better?'

The warmth of his embrace, the lack of any pressure in his words…some of Toni's tension eased. 'We don't have to be married for that,' she answered simply.

The dark eyes seemed to caress her soul with mesmerising gentleness as his voice caressed her mind with seductive thoughts. 'Toni, I don't want a some-time affair with you. I want you living with me. To wake in the morning with you beside me, and to run my fingers through your hair. To sit down at the dinner-table and have you sharing the meal with me. To see you. To experience you. To hear you talk and laugh. To listen to your ideas. To make love with you. Or, if you prefer me to put it another way, to have sex with you. To translate that into action. To share with you. Both of us... together. Whatever it is, I want it.'

He made it sound so good... being together... making love. Yet the words of a moment were translated into a lot of pain later on. She had to be careful. Total commitment—the kind he was offering her—that was for a lifetime. It made Toni feel very confused. He was painting a picture that appealed so much, yet... wouldn't he start making demands once his ring was on her finger? He would have expectations—men always did—and when she didn't live up to them, or when she wanted to go her own way and do her own thing...

'Noah, there are a lot of things I've planned to do with my life. Marriage was never very high on the list,' she started. 'I have ambitions and dreams.'

'Of course you have. And you must carry through on them,' he said reasonably. 'Maybe there are some I can share with you. Or help. I like your ideas on using the *wagons-lits* in Europe. I was wondering if you'd like to manage the overseas division——'

'Noah, I'd make a terrible wife. I'm no good at it!' she cut in desperately.

'I don't believe that,' he said with absolute certainty.

'I can't cook...'

'We can get over that problem fairly easily.'

'I hate housework...'

'None of that will apply to us, Toni,' he pointed out calmly. 'There's no need for you to cook or think of the laundry or do housework. I already have people who do all that. You'd be free to——'

'I don't like children!' she threw at him, forced into a partial untruth by the gathering force of his logic. And

logic didn't work in marriage. Things got all twisted
around. 'You know you want children,' she reminded
him vehemently. 'And I would be terrible with them.
What if I——?'

'It doesn't matter.'

'It does so matter!'

'Only you matter, Toni.'

'What if I'm infertile? What if——?'

'Toni, there isn't anything I wouldn't give, or give up,
to have you. However, if you decided some time in the
future, that you would like us to have a child, we could
get a nurse or a nanny so you wouldn't be tied down
with responsibilities you didn't want. In the end, it's your
body, and your decision——'

'But you really want children,' she broke in insis-
tently, reaching blindly for any reason to stop him from
wanting marriage with her.

He didn't flinch from the issue. 'Yes,' he said simply.

Perversely enough, his admission didn't make Toni
feel any better. She hadn't thought about children for
years—not really thought about them. There had come
a time where, on some subconscious level, she had not
wanted to have Murray's children. Although she had at
the beginning. Before... when she was too young and
inexperienced to know that ideas didn't always translate
into good realities.

But with Noah... She struggled against a dreadful
feeling of inevitability about what was going on. She
looked hard at Noah, urgently needing to reassess him.
It didn't seem to matter what argument she put up, he
was ready to tear it to shreds. Behind the soft caring in
his eyes, she sensed a rock-hard determination. She felt
she was floundering in a vacuum where there was nothing
to hold on to, and Noah was all around her, waiting for
her to emerge whichever way she turned.

'It won't work!' she cried in a last bleat of protest.

Then unaccountably, when he had her completely fenced in, when Toni was teetering on the edge of giving in because she hated the thought of giving him up, Noah calmly opened a door for her.

'If you're frightened to marry me, Toni, will you live with me? That way you can walk out any time you like. If it's not working for you.'

Relief rolled through her with the force of a mighty tidal wave. She could handle that. All her objections turned into meaningless flotsam and jetsam. She seized on his suggestion with joy in her heart and stars in her eyes.

'Yes,' she breathed ecstatically. 'I'll do that.'

She had been so tensed up herself that she hadn't realised that Noah had also been under considerable strain. He had spoken so calmly, been so...controlled... It wasn't until she saw his face relax, his mouth soften into a slow, happy smile, that she even began to comprehend how much her answer had meant to him. And then she wondered why he looked so pleased when it was supposed to be marriage that he had really wanted. She was almost sure it was triumph shining in his eyes. But it might simply be pleasure that they were going to be together.

He kissed her with slow sensuality. Toni couldn't help thinking she wouldn't mind having him kiss her like that every day. She had never considered living with a man before—apart from that abortive first marriage which had taught her how miserable it could be—but she really did feel it was worth trying with Noah. Not that she expected the arrangement to last long. She had no expectations of it at all. Except, if he kept making love to her as he was doing now, she wasn't at all sure where this would all end up.

Noah seemed to have lost all sense of responsibility, Toni thought, some considerable time later. The sunlight dappling through the latticed walls of the pergola was definitely that of late afternoon, and he still showed no inclination to get back to his guests. In fact, he seemed to have completely forgotten them.

Toni had no objection to his extremely pleasurable absorption in the texture of her skin. He had wonderfully sensitive fingertips. She didn't really feel much like reminding him of his duties as host—the deliciously sweet languor in her body was quite mind-sapping—but their long absence from the party might be disturbing Ray. She wasn't sure that her stepfather was all that confident about the rights of her meddling. As things had turned out, she could now prove to him that everything was fine, and Toni felt it behove her to set his mind at rest.

'Noah...' She grazed her fingertips over the incredibly sexy dimple just below the pit of his back.

'Mmm...' He gave a little shudder of pleasure.

Toni suspected that his mind wasn't concentrated at all. Noah was a terribly sensual person. She wondered how she had made the mistake of thinking him totally computerised.

'There are a whole lot of people up around your pool,' she told him. 'And you invited them. So you ought——'

'The only important person I invited was you,' he murmured, nuzzling her ear in the most distracting fashion.

Toni took a deep breath to neutralise the lovely quivery feeling. 'Noah, Jocelyn is important to me. And so is Ray. And he still thinks I don't like you very much,' she said as firmly as she could.

That seemed to do the trick of clicking his mind back into gear. He lifted his head and his eyes met hers with serious intent. 'I'll talk to him, Toni. As soon as we go back.'

'You don't have to do that, Noah. I'll——'

'Toni,' he was very serious, 'if you were my daughter, I'd want the man you're going to live with to lay his cards straight on the table. I want no misunderstanding with Ray about where I stand in this arrangement. You tell him whatever you wish. But I'd like you to let me speak to him first. It's a point of courtesy that means a lot to me.'

Toni could see that he meant it. While it sounded rather old-fashioned in this day and age, particularly since they weren't getting married, she found that she respected Noah's point of view. It was an admirable thing to do, and she knew Ray would respect Noah all the more for it. Toni liked that idea. Very much.

'All right,' she conceded happily. 'I'll talk to Jocelyn while you talk to Ray. Then we'll have everything settled.'

He gave her that grin that still left her befuddled with all sorts of emotions. It wasn't actually wicked at all, she decided. More a combination of delight and satisfaction and . . . triumph.

Toni shrugged off the thought, too happy with the situation to wonder too much about it. 'We've been here a long time,' she pointed out.

'You want to make a move?'

'I think so.'

He grinned again. 'That doesn't sound very definite.'

She laughed. 'What you do to me, Noah Seton, is rather addictive.'

'Good! I'd hate to be the only one addicted.'

'But we should go.'

'Whatever you say.'

It was a good thing their clothes had been made from non-crease materials, Toni thought as they set off back to the party, but she had an awful suspicion that she was wearing a glow that no one would have much difficulty in interpreting. Even Noah looked different somehow . . . his face very relaxed and his eyes shiny and indulgent.

They didn't exactly make fast progress back to the pool area. The urge to kiss her and hold her close overcame Noah every few metres, and Toni found it all too easy to forget where they were supposed to be going and what was supposed to be done. The garden at Summerfield Green was certainly an enchanting place. She was sure she would be very happy living here with Noah.

Eventually they reached the seventeenth-century Italian gates, and Noah managed to find enough sense of purpose to open one of them and let Toni pass through. His arm was around her waist again the moment he rejoined her, but then there were people hailing them as though they had been very much missed from the company. She and Noah exchanged a look of reluctant but mutual resignation, then separated to go about their designated tasks.

Ray had been consuming fine champagne at a pleasantly steady rate all afternoon. It had helped him through Richard Gilbert's request for Jocelyn's hand in marriage. He was quite proud of the way he had granted permission without so much as a quiver of concern in his voice. The young doctor was, at the very least, a gentleman. Not like that smooth con-artist who had lured Antonia into a marriage that made Ray shudder every time he thought of it. But there never had been any stopping Antonia when her mind was mind up.

The champagne had helped to soothe those discomfiting memories, but it hadn't quite allayed his concern over the fact that Antonia had disappeared with Noah

Seton soon after lunch and they had been gone a very long time indeed. To Ray's mind, running interference with a man like Noah Seton would demand as much care as picking a safe path through a mine-field. However, he had learnt never to underestimate Antonia. Compelling she was. Orthodox she wasn't. One just never knew what would happen. Which was why she made life so interesting.

However, despite the amount of champagne he had consumed, Ray's powers of perception remained as sharp as ever. The moment he saw Noah Seton reappear with Antonia, the signs were instantly recognisable. As unbelievable as it might seem, as unexpected as it was, there could be no doubt. Noah Seton had not only run into interference. He had been hit by a runaway train.

Ray felt a twinge of sympathy for the man. Of course, one grew accustomed to it in time. One could almost say addicted. Antonia was... Antonia. Ray straightened in his chair as Noah walked purposefully towards him. Obviously Noah Seton was a man with a mission on his mind. Ray had seen the same kind of expression on Richard Gilbert's face earlier on.

'Ray, I want to marry Toni,' he stated unequivocally, the moment he was settled face to face.

'Yes. I can see that,' Ray agreed affably, wondering if he could now forget about any charge of breaking good will. A man in love—as besotted as Noah Seton had looked a few moments ago...

'But she has some trauma about marriage that I can't get around at this particular point,' Noah continued, apparently undeterred by Antonia's refusal.

'Ah...' Ray said, frowning as he considered the possibilities. He was all too aware that there could be many reasons why Antonia would not accept Noah's proposal. He hoped that she had let the man down lightly.

On the other hand, Noah certainly didn't look as if he had been put off. 'Um...it's not that she doesn't like you?' Ray asked warily.

'That's no issue,' Noah dismissed, with so much confidence that Ray couldn't doubt it. 'Toni has agreed to try living with me. It's not an arrangement that I like announcing to you, but I intend to take whatever she will give me. I simply want you to know that I will care for her as though she were my wife, for as long as she will stay with me. And I hope that will be for the rest of our lives.'

Ray nodded as he absorbed the somewhat startling information. Antonia must have suddenly learnt to like Noah Seton a lot. But he could understand why she wouldn't want to commit herself into his keeping. Not lock, stock and barrel. Noah Seton was not the type of man who let go anything that he took over. She would be wary...leaping in too soon...after her last bad experience. And yet Ray had the feeling that Noah Seton would care for her in the ways that Murray Sheldon never had.

'Antonia had a bad time with her first marriage, Noah,' he warned kindly. 'I know you're cast from a different mould from Murray Sheldon, but if you want my advice...'

'I do,' Noah said emphatically, his eyes sharpening.

'Antonia is a very special person. I don't want to see her light dimmed again,' Ray said slowly, his own love for her filtering into his voice. 'Don't take too much, Noah. Don't be greedy. She needs...room...to be herself. If you just remember that *it's what Antonia is now* that has drawn you to her, then you'll know that to try and mould her into something else can only make you both unhappy.'

'I'll remember that,' Noah said quietly. 'Is there anything more specific about her first marriage which you——?'

Ray shook his head. 'That's Antonia's private business, Noah. And every relationship is different. Concentrate on what you can have with her. Don't bring up the past. It won't do you any good.'

'Thank you, Ray. I deeply appreciate what you've said. More than anything else in my life, I want Toni to be happy with me.'

'Then I wish you well, Noah. I hope it will be so. Antonia is very dear to me. And I'd like now to have a few private words with her, if you don't mind.'

'Of course.'

Ray watched him go to her. Antonia had been talking to Jocelyn, who looked somewhat stunned. The moment Noah appeared at Antonia's side, she looked up at him with such a vibrant light on her face that Ray felt tears prick at his eyes. Too much champagne, he thought, but it didn't deter him from taking another sip to ease the sudden lump in his throat.

Noah Seton had to be a man with enormous powers of persuasion, he concluded, and although he was well aware of the strength of Antonia's will he had a strong intuitive feeling that, if Noah was determined on marriage, it was all simply a matter of time.

The house was going to seem very empty without Antonia, he thought bleakly. But he would have Jocelyn for a while. And eventually there would be grandchildren. Jocelyn would be keen to have a baby almost as soon as she was married. And Richard didn't look as if he would deny her anything.

Antonia...and Noah... Would they ever have children? Ray hoped so. He sincerely hoped so. Somehow

it would be terribly wrong if they didn't. Like a denial
of the life he saw pulsing between them.

She turned towards him—the vivid tornado who had
whirled around him for so many memorable years—and
she walked with a light spring in her step, her curls
bouncing, her face coloured with that intense vivacity,
her mother's beautiful green eyes dancing with inner
excitement. Leonie had always been so proud of her
dynamic little girl, he thought for one brief, grieving
moment, then quickly steeled himself to give this dearly
beloved stepdaughter of his whatever she wanted or
needed from him.

'Ray . . .' she started, emanating decisive purpose even
as she smiled apologetically at him '. . . I know this must
be an incredible surprise to you . . .'

'Not at all,' he said with a grand dismissive gesture.
'I've been absorbing surprises ever since I arrived here.'
He smiled indulgently at her. 'In fact, I don't think I
can be surprised any more.'

She laughed and caught his hand, giving it a loving
squeeze before sitting down in the chair which Noah had
vacated. The laughter faded into a look of poignant
appeal. 'You do like him, Ray, don't you?'

The slight thread of uncertainty was an echo of that
former disastrous misjudgement when she had gone
against his advice and married Murray Sheldon. 'Yes,
Antonia. I think he's a man of integrity,' he said
solemnly.

She gave a self-conscious little laugh. 'Well, at least
he doesn't want me for my money. I haven't got any.'

Ray frowned. 'That's not strictly true, Antonia. In a
way—and I suppose it's time I confessed it to you—I
was at least partly responsible for the break-up of your
marriage with Murray Sheldon. I told him that all you
had was the trust money from your mother and that

Jocelyn was sole heiress to my estate. That he couldn't expect another cent as far as your connection to me was concerned.'

'Well, of course that's only right,' she expostulated. 'Jocelyn is——'

'Antonia...' He shook his head at her and his eyes begged her understanding. 'I lied for your sake, my dear. I hated to see him bleeding you in the ruthless, heartless way he did. And not just for the money. It had to stop. I had to stop it, you see. What he was doing to you...was too wrong. And it wasn't going to get better, no matter how hard you tried. You do see that now, don't you?'

'Yes,' she whispered.

'But, my dear little daughter—and you are that to me, as much as Jocelyn is,' he said gently, 'you stand to inherit equally with Jocelyn. And there are trust amounts put aside for various stages of your life. When you're thirty, and when——'

'Ray...' Tears blurred her eyes and she shook her head. 'I don't need it. I'll always cope with life. I'd rather it went to Jocelyn. Truly I would. You know I'd only mess it up anyway. I'm no good with money...'

'Then give it away, my dear. Whatever you want. I just wanted you to know that it is there for you. You don't ever have to stay with a man for the sake of security. You're free, Antonia. Free of any economic need, anyway.'

She quickly recovered herself and gave him a teasing little smile. 'I'm not going to live with Noah for his money, Ray.'

He cocked an enquiring eyebrow. 'It's a complete mystery to me why you are,' he said archly. 'You were only beginning to like him this morning.'

The laughter came back, beautifully uninhibited, just as he liked to hear it. 'Ray, he's the trickiest, most devious man alive. Which makes him a challenge all the time. But, even better than that, he makes love so beautifully I simply can't pass him up, not as long as he keeps on doing it. I did tell him it was only sexual attraction, Ray. I gave him fair warning...'

'All's fair in love and war,' he remarked evenhandedly. He had to admire Noah Seton for the gamble he had taken. As always with Antonia, the outcome was going to be very interesting. 'You know I only want what's best for you, my dear. If this is best, I wish you well with Noah Seton.'

She jumped up and hugged him. 'I knew you'd understand, Ray. I have to give it a try, don't I?'

'Nothing ventured, nothing gained,' he intoned.

'I do so love you,' she said, making it all worthwhile for him. Then she kissed his cheek and waltzed back to the man who had yet to hear those words from her lips. But the way she slipped happily into the eager crook of Noah Seton's arm said a lot. And the way Noah Seton's arm tightened around her said a lot more.

Tricky ... devious ... challenging ... committed ... and very, very determined!

Oh, yes...Ray could see an interesting few months coming up.

CHAPTER ELEVEN

LIFE with Noah was a continual surprise to Toni. He didn't criticise her at all. He didn't make demands. And he was incredibly virile. Not that she had any complaints about that. She had never felt so deliciously alive, right down to her toes! But she hadn't thought it was possible that any man would want to make love as much as Noah did. Which just went to show...there were always new things to learn. However, it was early days yet, she kept reminding herself. Although it was getting to be quite difficult to keep her feet on the ground, particularly around Noah.

He had a penthouse apartment at Circular Quay, right in the heart of the city, so that they didn't have to commute from Summerfield Green during the week to carry on with their work. Noah understood that she had to keep her employment agency going until she had placed every last person on her list. He even managed to find two more jobs to be filled in his own network of companies. Which was very helpful. In the end, it only took her a fortnight to bring her mission to a successful conclusion. The courier service with the refrigerated truck was incorporated into Ray's old transport company and everyone was happy.

Toni was a little awed when Noah showed her the extent of his business interests. She saw immediately that Ray's transport company was only a cog in a big wheel—an important cog, but not as important as she had thought. The possibilities of what could be done within Noah's larger sphere were tremendously exciting. She studied the overseas connections with avid interest. She had plenty of ideas. All that was lacking was a title to give herself.

'You haven't got a name for this position you're giving me, have you, Noah?' she tackled him one night.

'Not precisely,' he replied, drowning in the bright eagerness on her wonderful face. 'What would you suggest?'

'Well, I don't like President, Vice-President or Chairwoman...' Her smile dazzled him. 'I thought...Multiple Co-ordinating Controller. It has the sense of being important but helpful all at the same time. Is that all right with you?'

'Perfect!' he agreed without a second's thought. 'I'll have a title plate made up tomorrow. Cards printed...'

She bounced around the table and sat on his lap. 'You really do like my ideas, don't you?' she said elatedly.

'Brilliant,' he murmured, his gaze dropping to the provocative bow of her upper lip. He could feel himself stirring again. He had never been so stimulated in his life. Not even in his teens.

She laughed and jiggled around...and that was the end of another unfinished meal! Not that it mattered. He always enjoyed the midnight snacks they shared. He didn't even care about the occasional crumbs that got into their bed. Everything was fun with Toni. He couldn't remember ever having laughed so much as he did with her... He was enjoying being alive in a way he never thought possible before...and it certainly added another incredible dimension to making love.

Toni found that she was completely busy with her new job and all the other things that needed her attention. Jocelyn required help with organising her wedding to Richard. In the natural course of these preparations, the two stepsisters talked over a lot of aspects concerning the future in front of both of them, and Toni made some important decisions regarding her own life.

With the run-up to the auction there was much to do. Apart from the promotion, there were the prizes to organise. Although Lillian was making great strides there, she couldn't do without Toni's help. People had to be rallied and organised and persuaded. She found that dropping Noah Seton's name often had wonderful results. Moreover, a few ideas had to be injected into the programme to get it completely right. If they were auctioning fantasies, they had to be *great* fantasies.

It surprised her a little that Lillian had nothing to say about Toni's arrangement with Noah Seton. Everybody knew about it. It was a hot item around town, and there were even pictures of them in the newspapers. Not that that worried Toni. Her life was her own business, and 'living together' wasn't particularly scandalous any more.

However, she had expected at least a lifted eyebrow from Lillian, or a discreet question or two. After all, as they had agreed, men were pigs. But the only man Lillian talked about was Mr Templeton...what a marvellous cook he was...how kind and thoughtful and considerate for a man...so gentle and sweet... Toni began to wonder if Lillian was beginning to think sharing a bed with someone might not be such a bad thing. Of course, Mr Templeton could not be in the same class as Noah as a lover, but...who was to know whether or not he could satisfy Lillian's needs?

In any event the situation they needed for the auction was shaping up very well. There was no problem in talking Mr Templeton into his role. And Diana was stirring the pot in her usual brilliant way. So brilliantly, in fact, that what was happening drew a puzzled comment from Noah one evening.

'I can't understand it,' he said, shaking his head in bemusement. 'There are rumours going around Sydney and Melbourne about people who I know for a fact are as solid as the Bank of England. Yet I keep hearing that this one or that one is not as solvent as they look. It's absurd! I wonder what started it off...'

It was a good thing that Noah didn't read gossip columns, Toni thought, since her friendship with Diana Goldbach was fairly common knowledge. She wasn't too sure that Noah would approve of her tactics, although it was all in a good cause, she assured herself. A few dented egos were a minor suffering when compared to that of children who couldn't hear. Nevertheless, she felt that what Noah didn't know wouldn't hurt him. And she didn't want anything rocking the relationship they had.

So she changed the subject.

'Noah, I've been thinking about my job as Multiple Co-ordinating Controller...'

'Yes?' he asked.

It was tremendously pleasing the way he allowed himself to be diverted when she wanted him to be. His eyes zeroed in on her with totally absorbed concentration.

'Well, I really have a lot of activities that I'm interested in,' she explained. 'There's Jocelyn's wedding and various worthy charities that I get involved with from time to time. I don't see how I'm going to manage travelling overseas to supervise what has to be done while co-ordinating the transport there, yet——'

'You don't have to, Toni,' he said quickly. 'What you are, primarily, is a decision-maker. There are national managers to implement your decisions. All you have to do is spell them out.'

She beamed with pleasure. A decision-maker...she liked that. Yes, that was precisely what she was. And Ray had been quite right not to hand his business over to her. He had said at the time that it would demand too much from her and she wouldn't be free to do all the things she liked doing. He had also said she might get married again, and . . . She looked up at Noah and decided that there were some things she might have to rethink.

She smiled at him. 'Actually, I didn't like the thought of going away without, Noah. Living together is getting very addictive.'

He grinned.

And very shortly after that they ended up in bed again. Which was all extremely satisfactory. Certainly Noah forgot all about the rumours he had heard, and Toni decided she was never going to walk out on him, even though they hadn't been together for six weeks, let alone six months. Something this good could not change much. In fact, it just seemed to get better and better.

As Noah's fingertips grazed softly over her stomach, Toni wondered what it would be like to have his baby inside her. She imagined how pleased Noah would be. How happy she could make him if she gave him what he dearly wanted. After all, if he was committed to staying with her all his life—and Toni had no real doubt about that—it would be wrong to deprive him of having at least one heir to carry on his name and bloodline.

The days seemed to melt by in a haze of happiness. It was amazing how fast time went, with never a dull moment. Mr Templeton proved most amenable to the task Toni had in mind for him. He looked the part of a cultured man of wealth and prestige, and he was proud to serve.

'But if I'm to make these introductory bids, what happens if I get left with them? I haven't got the money to pay for them,' he pointed out.

'You can get caught once,' Toni explained. 'But only once! We simply pass that item back in and it will be auctioned off again at the end. The trick is to bid as high as possible and not get caught at all.'

'Ah!' he said, still obviously concerned about making a mistake.

'I'll be sitting next to you,' Lillian assured him. 'We've put a reserve price on all the prizes. I'll tell you when to stop.'

Mr Templeton relaxed, giving Lillian a soulful look. 'It is an honour and a privilege that you both entrust me with such deep confidence.'

Lillian glowed.

Toni judged it was time to leave them to it.

There wasn't much Toni didn't share with Noah, but she felt it was wiser to keep the trickier details about the auction to herself. However, for some reason Toni couldn't quite fathom, Noah became particularly interested in this charity event. He asked her for a list of all the fantasies that would be for sale and she brought home a copy of the catalogue that had been printed. He went over all the prizes with her—

there were nearly fifty—apparently curious to know if any had some special appeal to her.

'An afternoon with a famous artist who will do a pencil-portrait of you,' he read musingly. 'I wonder if he could capture you, Toni...' His eyes rested on her face a moment, then he shook his head and went back to the list. 'A walk-on part in a live opera performance...' His eyebrows lifted at her.

'I'd prefer to sing,' Toni said, wrinkling her nose at him.

He leaned over and kissed it. 'What about being a disc-jockey for two hours at a top radio station?' he persisted.

'Noah, I'm very happy with my life just the way it is,' she declared, hoping to discourage him from getting carried away at the actual auction. The bids were going to go awfully high if everything went according to plan, and, although Toni considered her stratagems perfectly justifiable, she wasn't sure Noah would see it that way if it cost him a lot of money.

He gave her that grin that raised flutters. 'Nothing that you'd particularly like? No dreams at all?'

'Not on that list.' She gave him back a provocative smile. 'The dream I have at the moment...is unprintable!'

Noah took the hint. It was one of the things Toni admired about him. She was getting to be so free with him that she hardly ever wore a bra any more, and sometimes not even panties. They just seemed to get in the way when she didn't want them there at all, and she derived a sneaking plesure from making Noah lose his control.

She wondered if Noah would still be virile right into his nineties like Charlie Chaplin. Maybe they would end up with loads of children. Somehow the idea had an appeal that threatened to supersede all her former preconceptions. It could very well be a lot of fun. She imagined a whole string of boys like Noah, and girls like herself, running through the gardens at Summerfield Green and playing all sorts of marvellous games. It was a super place for hide-and-seek. And Noah could teach them how to swim... Toni kept elaborating on these thoughts and they turned into a lovely dream.

Jocelyn's and Richard's wedding was like a lovely dream too. It was a stupendous affair, held in the beautiful grounds of Ray's home. It set Toni to thinking about herself and Noah. Here, in her mother's garden, was where they had first started to know each other, and after the two months they had spent together she didn't think there could be much left that she didn't know about him. It had been... quality time... which was far more important than quantity time. She hoped Jocelyn was going to be as happy with Richard as she was with Noah.

'The Charity Event Of The Year'—as some newspapers billed it—came fast on the heels of Jocelyn's wedding. It was definitely a night for flamboyance and style. All in all, if things went as planned Toni figured it would also be a night for celebration. She couldn't resist dressing in the scarlet satin she had been saving for just such an occasion.

After all Diana's subtle work, and if the tycoons had their egos imbedded in their hearts, arteries ought to start bursting everywhere. Therefore, scarlet was most appropriate. Besides, the colour went spectacularly well with Noah's formal black dress suit. He looked so stunningly handsome that she had to redo her lipstick before they could get on their way.

The ballroom at the Regent Hotel was decorated with moons and stars and clouds with silver linings. A huge tinselly banner ran above the stage—'Make Your Fantasy Come True!' Every woman Toni saw was decked out in diamonds and a designer dress. Every man looked bullishly determined. The stage was definitely set.

The dinner was an elaborate affair—as it should be, considering the price everyone was paying for it. Toni and Noah sat with Ray and Jocelyn and Richard. They had all come to see the fun rather than get involved with the bidding. Lillian and Mr Templeton were at a table which was closer to the stage, but was positioned so that most of the crowd was in ready view.

Toni noted that Mr Templeton looked very distinguished in the formal suit that had been hired for the occasion. Lillian, of course, was the picture of artless femininity in flowing chiffon. Diana Goldbach, sleekly dangerous in gold lamé, sat with them, although she didn't do much sitting during dinner. She table-hopped with artful purpose, flashing Toni a Cheshire Cat grin as she passed by. Her trail around the ballroom could be measured by the rise of aggression in the atmosphere.

It was markedly apparent, very early on, that cost was no object on this night of nights. The prestigious wines of the world flowed to the extent that the hotel would probably have to replenish its cellars in a very short period of time. There was a spontaneous burst of eager applause when the auctioneer finally took the microphone on stage. The tycoons were more than ready to strut their status.

The first item—a starring role in a television commercial for a Hunter River Valley winery—established a price-level in bids that floored even Toni. She was appalled when Mr Templeton calmly waved his catalogue twice, pushing the price higher and higher when it had already gone far beyond her expectations.

And Lillian had nudged him! Lillian had a suspiciously high flush on her face! Had she succumbed to her partiality for sherry and had one or two too many? Perhaps to screw her courage to the sticking point? Except this wasn't courage. Not even Dutch courage! It was downright recklessness!

By the tenth item, Toni seriously began to question what she had unleashed. Pandemonium reigned. People were shouting bids as if there were no tomorrow. The auctioneer had caught the fever and had moved into a combination of hot-gospelling and hysteria-selling. Mr Templeton, urged on by Lillian in some incredible lunacy, was leading the charge. Diana was flashing around, gleefully taking notes on who bought what. Buyers were positively preening over the madness of their purchases.

Jocelyn's eyes were as big as golf balls at the sums of money being raised. Richard kept shaking his head in dazed disbelief. Ray was chortling to himself as if this was the most entertaining night of his life. At least Noah was containing himself, Toni thought in some relief. It was a comfort to know that the father of her child was a sane, sensible man.

And that was a fact of which she was now quite sure. After tonight was over, she would tell him and then they would get married, just as he wanted to. She was certain in her mind now that Noah would make a very different husband from Murray Sheldon.

Perhaps it was her pregnancy that was causing her to feel quite faint in this overheated manic atmosphere. The blood-red haze in the ballroom was beginning to be nauseating. The auction was drawing to an end. There were only three items left to go, but suddenly Toni felt she had to get out of here and breathe in some cooler fresh air. She touched Noah's arm.

'Just going to the powder room,' she excused.

He nodded and she quickly left the table. She did not go to the powder room. She simply sat down on a chair in the foyer outside the ballroom and recollected herself with a few deep breaths. Perhaps it had been the cigar-smoke that had made her feel queasy. She was very glad that Noah didn't smoke cigars.

Once she felt a bit better, Toni wandered along the balcony which ran around the grand entrance foyer. The windows looked out over Circular Quay. She could even spot Noah's penthouse apartment at the top of one of the tall buildings that crowded around the quay. The lights of the city and the harbour seemed to soothe some of her inner turbulence.

The total of the proceeds of the auction had run into millions, even before she'd left. It was an astronomical success. Every deaf child in Australia who needed a bionic ear operation would now be able to get it.

She hoped that using Mr Templeton as a stimulus to increase the bidding would never become common knowledge. Not that it really mattered. After all, if those tycoons didn't have such colossal egos they could have let Mr Templeton win. They could have proved they had money left in the bank some other way. They didn't actually have to make such a terribly ostentatious display of their wealth.

On the other hand, while she had meant to bleed them, she hadn't meant them to spill this much blood. However, the fault was not all hers. Why was it that, when she planned things with the best intentions in the world, they sometimes took on a life of their own and got out of control?

She heard a step behind her. Without turning she knew it would be Noah. 'Are you all right, Toni?'

It was him.

She swung around and smiled away his concern. 'It got a bit close in there,' she explained. 'Is the auction over?'

'Just about. I gave the last item a miss and came looking for you.' He grinned. 'I bought the picnic.'

'The picnic?' Toni felt faint again.

'The gourmet picnic lunch complete with butler, waiters and chamber orchestra,' he elaborated—as if she didn't know. 'I knew you would love it. It's so romantic,' he said softly, and then a wry little smile curled his lips. 'There was some lunatic who kept bidding against me. In the end it cost me two hundred and twenty-five thousand dollars, but the publicity will be good for us and the company.'

He drew her into his arms, his eyes sparkling with some secret anticipation. 'You and I are going to have a right royal time of it, my darling. I wanted to give you something special. Very special. Because you are very, very special to me. And I wanted to show you that in a very concrete way.'

'Oh, Noah!' It was just as well he was supporting her in his embrace, because Toni was further weakened by a turbulent rush of emotion. There was a wave of guilt that he too had been caught up in the madness she had promoted, but overwhelming even that was a wave of intense feeling that she couldn't define at all. Except it was all connected to the kind of wonderful man he was. 'You give me too much,' she choked out, her throat almost blocked by a huge lump of something. 'You shouldn't have done that.'

'Toni! Toni!' The excited hail was from Lillian Devereux as she came sailing along the balcony, her face rosier than it had ever been in her teens, her brown eyes lit with magnificent dollar signs. 'We've made millions! Three million, nine hundred and eighty-seven thousand, six hundred and twenty-five dollars! Just think of that, you wonderful girl! I can't believe it! And we'd never have done it without you.'

Toni couldn't help smiling at Lillian's delight. 'Never set your sights too low,' she advised. 'Next time, Lillian, go for the big five.'

'The big five?'

'Five million.'

'You *are* wonderful, Toni!' Lillian gushed. She looked archly at Noah. 'It was all Toni's idea. I do hope you appreciate what a genius she is!'

'I do,' he said agreeably. 'I do, I do,' he added for good measure.

'It's so nice to have a man who is appreciative,' Lillian rattled on. 'My Arthur is wonderfully appreciative. We're getting married.'

'Arthur? Married?' Toni echoed, too bewildered by Lillian Devereux's announcement to make sense of anything. 'Who is Arthur?'

'Arthur...Arthur Templeton. Wasn't he magnificent tonight? The way he bid without fear...' There were stars in Lillian's eyes. 'And he didn't get caught even once!'

'Templeton...' Noah murmured as if it struck some chord in his memory. 'That name seems oddly familiar. Where have I heard it before——?'

It was time for a master-stroke...before another word was uttered! 'Noah,' said Toni decisively. 'If

Lillian is getting married . . . you're going to have to marry me.'

It concentrated his mind wonderfully. 'Do you mean that?' he asked incredulously.

'I never say what I don't mean,' Toni declared emphatically. 'Except by mistake.'

Lillian patted Noah's arm. 'You really should marry her.'

'I will. I'm going to. As soon as she lets me,' Noah said hastily. His eyes held a glazed look, and before he could say any more to Toni, Ray and Diana Goldbach descended upon them.

The balcony was getting very crowded, Toni thought, but at least Lillian drifted away, presumably back to the all-dangerous Arthur.

'Ah! You're all right, Antonia,' Ray said.

'Toni, give me a call whenever you want help,' Diana said, patting her back gleefully as she passed by. 'I'm off to write the story of the year. It will certainly mean a promotion for me. Apart from which, I haven't enjoyed myself so much in years.' She rolled her eyes as she waved goodbye. 'And that Mr Templeton . . .'

'Templeton . . .' Noah frowned.

Toni just knew he was going to put it altogether any second now, and he had paid all that money . . . and her future was at stake!

'Noah, I'm sick! Very sick!' she declared in desperation.

A startled look lifted the frown. 'What's wrong?' he asked with admirable simplicity.

'I've made the Ultimate Sacrifice!' she said. 'For you! I've got morning sickness at night!'

His face underwent another change, becoming suffused with the warmest glow. 'You're going to have a baby?'

'I'm totally, irrevocably and thoroughly pregnant!' she said. 'And *I* know that *you* are the *cause* of *it*.'

He looked extremely proud of himself...of her...of everything. 'That's wonderful! We'll get married straight away. Tomorrow. Tonight...'

'You're going to have to look after me, Noah,' Toni demanded.

'I will,' he said with fervour. 'I will, I will, I will.'

'You're going through this pregnancy as no man has ever gone through a pregnancy before.'

'Yes,' he agreed.

'You'd better make it good if this is to be only the first of your children.'

'As good as I can make it,' he promised.

She sighed contentedly, then gave him a blatant invitation with her eyes. 'Make my toes curl, Noah.'

He kissed her senseless.

'Let's go home,' he murmured raggedly, his eyes dark whirlpools of adoring desire.

'Yes,' she breathed, her whole being yearning to be joined with him for all eternity. And she silently vowed she would never hold secrets from him again. Not about anything!

Ray watched them go without a word. To break into the beauty of that moment would have been something approaching sacrilege. Congratulations could wait. He smiled to himself as he went back into the ballroom to rejoin Jocelyn and Richard. Noah had looked as if he had been hit by a runaway train again.

No doubt about Antonia, Ray thought with indulgent pride. She could swing a surprise with maximum impact any time at all. Noah obviously

hadn't got to his second proposal. And there was going
to be a grandchild much sooner than Ray had
expected. He tried to imagine the kind of child that
Antonia and Noah would produce. An earth-shaker,
he decided. A little earth-shaker. He or she could be
nothing less.

CHAPTER TWELVE

NOAH was kissing Toni beautifully when the door-chimes rang through the penthouse apartment. He reluctantly lifted his lips away from the fascinating attraction of hers and took a deep breath.

'God knows who it can be at this hour, but I'll answer that darling. You get out of your clothes and lie down. It's been a very taxing night for you,' he added, belatedly remembering her morning sickness. 'Would you like me to bring you a drink? Something to eat?'

'No. I'm much better now.' She smiled her siren smile. 'Please hurry back, Noah. Carrying this baby of yours, I'm not going to be beautiful much longer.'

He took another deep breath and forced himself to leave her. She was actually going to have his child, he thought blissfully as his feet automatically found their way to the front door. The first—only the first—of his children. If he looked after her properly. That was what she had said. And she was going to marry him. He could hardly believe it...though he couldn't doubt her. Toni never said anything she didn't mean.

He opened the front door to a man he had never seen before in his life. He introduced himself as some kind of estate agent, said he'd finally tracked Antonia Braden down, knew she was living here, and demanded to see her. He had a writ to serve. She owed a month's rent on an office. He was not going to wait. Bring her forth, he demanded. He intended to serve the notice. He had obligations to fulfil.

'How much does she owe?' Noah asked, recollecting that Toni freely admitted she was no good with money. Ideas were her strong point. And he had no argument about either facet of such a marvellous, incredible woman. Who was going to be his wife. Who was almost his wife right now.

'You're talking about my wife,' he said with steely authority. 'So be very careful what you say.'

The agent looked suitably taken aback. 'The money...'

'Come and see me on Monday. I'll fix it up then.' He didn't give a damn what Toni cost him. If he had to make a fortune every day of his life to keep her, he'd do it. Then he remembered another thing she had said. 'By the way, that building where the office is—I'm interested in buying it. Work out a deal.' He gave the agent his card. 'If you can come up with the right price, we can do business together.'

'You want to buy it?' the agent repeated, not quite believing his ears. He had come to collect a debt and he was having a commission dangled in front of his eyes as he had never envisaged in his whole career of letting rooms!

'If the price is right,' Noah affirmed. 'My wife...' she was virtually his and it sounded so good to say it '...tells me it will be an important building one day. I'm inclined to believe her.'

'Yes...yes,' the agent agreed eagerly. After all, if his wife was Antonia Braden, she could make a man believe anything. Perhaps she was right anyway. Maybe it would be an important building one day. It was worthwhile thinking about it. In any event, since he was going to get his money, he was not about to argue about the building. 'Goodnight, sir. Thank you, sir. I'll see you Monday, sir,' he said, and left while the going was good.

Noah closed the door. He felt very pleased with himself. He would give Toni the building too. But first the emeralds. He went to the wall-safe and took out the jeweller's box. He had meant to use the picnic as the occasion to propose to her once more. He had bought the emeralds to add persuasion to his suit for marriage. Toni had messed up his timing again, but this was much better than any plan he had ever made.

He laughed softly to himself as the reason for her timing clicked into place. Mr Templeton... Lillian Devereux... Diana Goldbach. Toni's Mr Templeton had been the plant at the auction, and the whole devious—but brilliant—build-up to the night had Toni's fingerprints all over the whole operation. He had been very slow to cotton on to what had been happening. Toni... He grinned. What a tricky, wonderfully challenging woman she was! He would, of course, never let on what he knew. Two hundred and twenty-five thousand dollars he had paid for that picnic...

'Noah... it's very lonely in this big bed all by myself,' Toni cried out plaintively.

Worth every cent of what he had paid, Noah thought with satisfaction. Almost a bargain, really. He headed back to the bedroom. She was sprawled across the bed, stark naked, and his pulse instantly leapt into overdrive. He put the jeweller's box down on the dressing-table and stripped off his clothes. The way Toni watched him excited him even more.

'You beat all the statistics, Noah,' she said appreciatively. 'I like to feel your muscles.'

Noah knew he wasn't built like Mr Universe. He was strong, but nothing unique. Nevertheless, if Toni liked to think he was, Noah was not about to correct her. Perhaps he should start working out at a gym.

'How did you manage to get pregnant so quickly?' he asked, still amazed that she had allowed it to happen.

'It wasn't supposed to happen this quickly. How could I possibly know you were so potent that you'd turn all the medical averages upside-down? Some people try to have babies for months. Years! It's all your fault, Noah. And now you have to pay the penalty,' she said archly.

He laughed and handed her the jeweller's box. 'Will this do for starters?'

She opened the box and her gasp of surprised delight was music to his ears. 'For me? Oh, Noah! This isn't looking after me ... this is out and out spoiling!'

He sprawled beside her and lifted out the ring. 'First, this one ...' He slid it on her finger. 'Now, you're formally betrothed to me.' He handed her the earrings to put on. 'These are to match your eyes.' Then he took up the necklace and fastened it around her throat. 'And this is for being so generous to me,' he concluded softly, his eyes loving her for giving him his child.

She took a deep breath. Then softly, simply, she said, 'I love you, Noah.' And in her eyes was the reflection of what he felt for her, and he knew in that moment a sense of utter completeness that he would hold within him for the rest of his life.

'I love you, Antonia,' he replied, hoping she would not deny him this time.

'Yes. I know,' she said softly, and held out her arms to him. 'But all my friends call me Toni.'

'The people who love you most deeply call you Antonia,' he said simply.

It was a beautiful thing to say. Noah was like that, Toni thought, revelling in her love for him, and his for her. She wondered why it had taken her so long to accept what they really felt for each other. But that didn't matter now.

They had made love countless times, but this was the best ever, from beginning to end, and even the peaceful aftermath held a very special bliss as they lay contentedly in each other's arms.

'Noah, you're going to have to share this pregnancy completely with me,' Toni suddenly declared. 'I might not be very good at it. I haven't had any practice.'

He smiled in the darkness. 'Is that supposed to be a penalty?'

'Well, you made it happen before I was really ready,' she argued.

'Does it worry you?' he asked.

She sighed and snuggled closer. 'Not if you look after me.'

He kissed the wild unruly curls away from her temples. 'I'll look after you. Always.'

'Mmm...' It was a hum of pleasure. 'How many children would you like to have, Noah?'

'However many you want,' he answered, not even pausing to think.

It was this woman in his arms he wanted most of all . . . flesh of his flesh, heart of his heart, soul of his soul. He listened to her muse over various numbers of children, agreeing with everything she said, knowing that she would always be the centre of his existence. Undoubtedly she would shake the earth around him innumerable times, as she had done from the moment he had first set eyes on her, but he would never want to live without her.

She was . . . would always be . . . his wife!

COMPELLING FINAL CHAPTER

EDEN – Penny Richards   **£2.99**

The final novel in this sensational quartet tracing the
lives of four very different sisters.
After helping her younger sisters to find love. Eden
felt she'd missed her own chance of happiness.
Then Nick Logan blew into her life like a breath of
fresh air! His young good-looks threatened her
respectable reputation – but if this was her one
chance at love, Eden was determined to take it.

July 1990

W●RLDWIDE

DON'T MISS OUT ON HOLIDAY ROMANCE!

Four specially selected brand new novels from popular authors in an attractive easy-to-pack presentation case.

THE TIGER'S LAIR
Helen Bianchin
THE GIRL HE LEFT BEHIND
Emma Goldrick
SPELLBINDING
Charlotte Lamb
FORBIDDEN ATTRACTION
Lilian Peake

This year take your own holiday romance with you.

Look out for the special pack from 29th June, 1990 priced £5.40.

Zodiac Wordsearch
Competition

How would you like a years supply of Mills & Boon Romances ABSOLUTELY FREE?

Well, you can win them! All you have to do is complete the word puzzle below and send it into us by Dec 31st 1990. The first five correct entries picked out of the bag after this date will each win a years supply of Mills & Boon Romances (Six books every month - worth over £100!) What could be easier?

S	E	C	S	I	P	R	I	A	M	F
I	U	L	C	A	N	C	E	R	L	I
S	A	I	N	I	M	E	G	N	S	R
C	A	P	R	I	C	O	R	N	U	E
S	E	I	R	A	N	G	I	S	I	O
Z	O	D	W	A	T	E	R	B	R	I
O	G	A	H	M	A	T	O	O	A	P
D	R	R	T	O	U	N	I	R	U	R
I	I	B	R	O	R	O	M	G	Q	O
A	V	I	A	N	U	A	N	C	A	C
C	E	L	E	O	S	T	A	R	S	S

Pisces	Aries	Leo	Earth	
Cancer	Gemini	Virgo	Star	**Please turn over for entry details**
Scorpio	Taurus	Fire	Sign	
Aquarius	Libra	Water	Moon	
Capricorn	Sagittarius	Zodiac	Air	

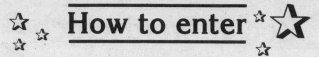

☆ How to enter ☆

All the words listed overleaf, below the word puzzle, are hidden in the grid. You can can find them by reading the letters forwards, backwards, up and down, or diagonally. When you find a word, circle it, or put a line through it. After you have found all the words, the left-over letters will spell a secret message that you can read from left to right, from the top of the puzzle through to the bottom.

Don't forget to fill in your name and address in the space provided and pop this page in an envelope (you don't need a stamp) and post it today.   Competition closes Dec 31st 1990.

Only one entry per household (more than one will render the entry invalid).

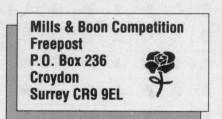

Mills & Boon Competition
Freepost
P.O. Box 236
Croydon
Surrey CR9 9EL

Hidden message _____

_____

Are you a Reader Service subscriber.   Yes ☐   No ☐

Name_____

Address_____

_____

_____

_____ **Postcode**_____

You may be mailed with other offers as a result of entering this competition.
If you would prefer not to be mailed please tick the box. No ☐   COMP9